THE MAN ON HORSEBACK

Also by Pierre Drieu la Rochelle

Ghost Light (Le Feu Follet)

THE MAN ON HORSEBACK

by

PIERRE DRIEU LA ROCHELLE

Translated by
Thomas M. Hines

First published in 1943 as *L'Homme à Cheval*
Translation © 1978 Summa Publications
This edition © 2020 Rogue Scholar Press
All Rights Reserved

ISBN: 978-1-954357-05-1

TABLE OF CONTENTS

"Cursed be he who would remain silent in the middle of the
wilderness, thinking that no one could hear his voice ..."

Balzac *(Séraphita)*

INTRODUCTION

The author of our novel, Pierre Drieu la Rochelle, is virtually unknown to the English-speaking public—with the notable exception of university scholars who specialize in modern French literature or political history. In France and Europe, however, his reputation as a first-rate novelist and political theorist has long been firmly established. Even today, more than three decades after his death, Drieu's major works are still in print and are registering moderate but consistent sales. Within the last fifteen years, four of his novels and one short story collection have been reissued in pocketbook format, demonstrating his popularity with the general public.

Yet, in spite of critical acclaim and widespread recognition as a creative artist, Drieu remains a controversial figure in modern French letters. His militant commitment to fascism coupled with the active role he played as a collaborator during the German occupation of Paris from 1940 to 1944 still evoke hostile reactions in certain quarters. Other opponents, mellowing with age, have tended to forgive these wartime transgressions. Moreover, with the coming of a new generation, the virulent passions that once surrounded Drieu's name have weakened considerably.

While it is possible for us to reject categorically Drieu's political views, we can hardly remain indifferent to his search for a meaningful existence through literature and art. If, indeed, the chances for survival of a writer's work can be measured in part by the degree to which he prods and questions the reader's conventional values and beliefs, the majority of Drieu's writings should easily withstand the test of time. It is no exaggeration to say that Drieu was one of the most prophetic and representative novelists of his generation. Together with other men of action such as Malraux, Saint-Exupéry, and Montherlant, Drieu stands at the forefront of the movement called "committed literature" (*la littérature engagée*) that flourished during the thirties and forties, culminating with the exponents of existentialism in the post-war years.

Because of the heavily autobiographical nature of Drieu's novels, we would like to present first of all a chronological synopsis of his life and major works. Hopefully, this will promote a better understanding of *The Man on Horseback* in which the author's life and his creation are inextricably, even symbiotically linked. The novel, moreover, is a striking illustration of Drieu's tendency to use literature as a means of self-exploration and vicarious fulfillment. *The Man on Horseback* is also a reflection, within an allegorical framework, of the political and ideological crises of the times. In this respect, it can be labeled a novel of "testimony" *(roman de témoignage)* on both a personal and societal level. Although *The Man on Horseback* cannot be fully explicated or judged on the basis of external references alone, it can be understood as a total work of art only by taking into consideration its autobiographical dimension.

Pierre-Eugène Drieu la Rochelle was born in Paris on January 3, 1893. Both parents were of Norman extraction and solidly middle-class in their upbringing and attitudes. As a child, Drieu regularly spent his summer vacations along the coast of Normandy and Brittany where he developed a love for swimming, the only sport at which he excelled. His father was an unsuccessful businessman—charming but weak-willed—whom Drieu admittedly despised and feared. Within his family, adultery and a long series of financial crises were constant sources of discord and bitterness. For years Drieu was haunted by the specter of his father's inadequacies and ultimate failure. As a result, one of the essential themes of his writings was the need to be free of a repressive heritage and prove to himself that he could overcome those character flaws inherited from his father and exacerbated by an unstable childhood. Very early in life—as he later confessed in his essay, *Récit secret (Secret Tale)*—Drieu had toyed with the idea of suicide, even going so far as to prick his chest with a paring knife until he bled. Years later, after the Liberation of Paris and months of seclusion, this pervasive urge toward self-destruction would finally be realized.

In keeping with the orthodox conservatism of his family, Drieu attended a parochial high school, run by the Marist order, where he distinguished himself as a brilliant student. During these formative years, he tried his hand at writing in several genres under the tutelage of an older acquaintance, Raoul Dumas, who professed an admiration for the nineteenth-century Parnassian school of poetry. After receiving his *baccalauréat* or high school diploma, Drieu entered the prestigious Ecole des Sciences Politiques in Paris and also enrolled at the Sorbonne where he majored in English. Although everyone, classmates and professors alike, had assumed he would graduate at the very top of his class, Drieu failed his final qualifying examinations and was consequently prevented from fulfilling his dreams of a diplomatic career.

Embittered by this failure, Drieu waived his student deferment and enlisted in the infantry. When war broke out with Germany in 1914, Drieu's unit was one of the first to see action near the small town of Charleroi in Belgium. During this battle—which in truth was hardly more than an extended skirmish—Drieu experienced a revelation of almost mystical proportions which touched the very core of his being. While his company was pinned down by enemy fire, Drieu spontaneously rallied his fellow soldiers and led them in a bayonet charge against the German machine-gun nest. By this act of heroism, Drieu came forcefully into contact with an aspect of his personality he had never encountered before—a latent dionysiac vitality which had been held in check by an overly rational education. Throughout his entire life, Drieu looked back on this moment as one of extraordinary importance. Instead of the physically inept intellectual he had thought himself to be, Drieu became during this confrontation with death a natural-born leader—*un vrai chef*. This merging of the contemplative and dynamic selves (reminiscent of the Nietzschean Apollonian-Dionysian dichotomy) created within Drieu a sense of oneness, of being momentarily a *complete* individual. Action and thought had coalesced into meaningful, indelible acts that shaped the world around him. Without question, Drieu's quest for self-identity can be traced to this episode of manly and spiritual awakening at the battle of Charleroi.

Wounded three times, incapacitated as well by a severe case of dysentery during the Dardanelles campaign, Drieu spent the rest of the war intermittently at the front and in the hospitals of the rear.

During the post-war period, Drieu became a fashionable and much-discussed author whose associations ran the gamut from the flamboyant anarchism and revolt of the Surrealists to the ultra-conservative ranks of Charles Maurras' Action Française and its monarchistic tenets.

Although Drieu first achieved recognition as a poet (*Interrogation*, 1917, his collection of war poems, is still highly regarded by critics), he quickly adopted the novel and essay as his preferred means of expression. His initial efforts at writing fiction were predictably awkward and somewhat erratic. Typical of most young writers, Drieu chose to portray aspects of his own life in his first "novel," *Etat civil* (*Vital Statistics*), 1921. Mixing autobiographical references and childhood fantasies, Drieu compiled the first of his many fictional counterparts, young Cogle, rebellious child of the times. In this work, Drieu enunciated a primary theme of his writings—the yearning to be free from the bonds of a prescribed social and psychological identity. Like young Cogle, later protagonists in Drieu's novels would seek to go beyond the cumbersome weight of family heritage in order to achieve a new self-perception.

In 1922 Drieu's first book-length essay appeared, *Mesure de la France* (*A Close Look at France*), and his reputation as a provocative and controversial political analyst was immediately established. Contrary to popular opinion, Drieu warned his countrymen that victory over the Germans had not been exclusively a French triumph but the result of the timely intervention of foreign powers on their side. The inability of the French to control their destiny as a nation was caused, Drieu believed, by a profound decadence which had afflicted every aspect of society. In his eyes, the most deplorable signs of this lack of individual and national vitality were a declining birth rate and the attendant repercussions upon France's role as a world leader.

In his second novel, *L'Homme couvert de femmes* (*The Ladies' Man*), 1925, Drieu mercilessly dissects the moral emptiness and sexual excesses of the post-war generation in France. In this denunciation of the gilded youth of the "Roaring Twenties," Drieu forged a style of writing that would become closely identified with his fiction: unfailingly tasteful, his novels were nonetheless negative in tone and harshly critical of society and the author himself. As an active participant in the drama of his era, Drieu infused his works with a spirit of personal commitment and undeniable sincerity. His truculence and urbane cynicism only served to mask a feeling of pervasive despair. The motivating force behind his literary activity was undoubtedly his quest for self-identity and a unified personality. As Drieu later explained in the autobiographical essay, "L'itinéraire," he had always considered his inner self to be fertile ground for literary experimentation. By isolating certain of his own attributes (primarily negative ones) within various fictional characters, he could then manipulate and observe the interplay of these qualities and possibly arrive at a deeper understanding of his psyche through this method of self-analysis. Each novel, therefore, would portray a new but evanescent image of the author in search of himself.

One drawback to this autobiographical approach to literature was the inevitable tendency on the part of the reader to see in these fictional counterparts little more than a cleverly altered mirror-image of Drieu himself. In spite of the demonstrable artistry of his narrative technique and characterizations, Drieu would long be denied the title of authentic novelist. For later generations—and in some respects even today—Drieu would be the dissolute womanizer of *The Ladies' Man*, more libertine than dedicated artist, supremely callous and exploitative in his dealings with the opposite sex. Yet the fictional Drieu—i.e., the side of his personality he delineated in such unflattering terms—cannot be totally affiliated with the private Drieu. Rather than simple reflections of their creator, Drieu's characters were essentially prismatic in composition and effect. Although reasonably faithful to real-life prototypes, they would take on different shapes and colorations once engaged in the flow of action and subjected to the exigencies of plot and dramatic tempo. Fictional autobiography, therefore, was not so much a self-indulgent or narcissistic mode of expression as it was a genuine effort on Drieu's part to capture the essence of an entire generation through self-examination. In this capacity as a witness of his times, Drieu has been compared to the American expatriate writers of the post-war era, in particular Fitzgerald and Hemingway. Just as *The Sun Also Rises* heralded a new sensibility in American letters, *The Ladies' Man* was a work of ground-breaking dimensions as well in its portrayal of a new European *mal du siècle*—a sense of moral and spiritual void in a world fragmented by war and social alienation.

Although Drieu continued to write fiction during the late twenties and early thirties, his attention was turned more and more toward politics. In two major essays during this period—*Genève ou Moscou* (*Geneva or Moscow*), 1928, and *L'Europe contre les patries* (*Europe Against National Boundaries*), 1931—Drieu warned prophetically that the revival of nationalistic passions throughout Europe would only impede the creation of a unified continent. As a confederation of states (similar to the Helvetian model), Europe could then promote its best interests by counterbalancing the growing influence of the youthful American and Russian empires. Divided into opposing national groups, however, the nations of Europe would be unable to resist the "imperialistic" designs of American capitalism and Soviet communism. In this respect, it is worth noting that more than thirty years later the well-known French magazine editor and politician, Jean-Jacques Servan-Schreiber, in his best-selling book, *Le Défi américain* (*The American Challenge*), would dramatically catalog the extent to which American technocratic know-how had dangerously eroded both French and European autonomy in critical areas by a form of economic colonization—a trend that Drieu had intuitively grasped and decried years before.

During the thirties in France and throughout Europe, political parties were polarized along strict ideological lines—even more so, perhaps, than in previous eras. As the French parliament became more sympathetic to socialistic ideals and programs, the conservative forces grew progressively more hostile to the government. In February 1934, loosely organized but rebellious right-wing elements marched across the Place de la Concorde in Paris and attempted to storm the National Assembly where the parliament was in session. The rioters were driven back only after a bloody confrontation with the police in which many people were killed. Prior to witnessing this abortive *putsch*, Drieu had only toyed with the prospect of committing himself to a political cause for the purpose of mixing "ink with blood"—i.e., testing the validity of his ideas in authentic situations. Having been impressed by the revolutionary fervor of the anti-parliamentarian groups and sensing as well that the time had come for him to take a public stand on political matters, Drieu professed his allegiance to fascism in a collection of perceptive essays, *Socialisme fasciste*, that appeared several months after the February riots. According to Drieu, there was no other acceptable alternative to either capitalistic or communistic dominance in Europe except the fascist ideology and its promises of national autonomy within a European confederation of fascist states.

To a certain degree, this clarion call of an authoritarian existence can best be understood in light of the widespread disillusionment many Frenchmen experienced with parliamentary democracy and its apparent inefficiency in dealing with problems of rapid social change and chronic governmental instability. Conversely, fascism promised an end to insecurity by proposing a structured society of well-defined limits, charismatic leadership, autocratic government and the revitalization, both moral and physical, of European man himself. Although it claimed to be revolutionary and future-oriented, fascism was at best a reactionary ideology that sought to reinstate the corporative economy and martial values of the Middle Ages within contemporary Europe. Its mythology reflected a nostalgic yearning for a more orderly world—a golden age in which social unrest would be neutralized by governmental and institutional rigidity. Under the fascist regime, man would no longer be fragmented but made whole again—a total being, cleansed of decadence and liberated from the "tyranny" of Cartesian thought and its scientific offspring, rationalism. Thus, for reasons we shall investigate more thoroughly in our discussion of *The Man on Horseback*, Drieu rejected the egalitarian spirit and objectives of the Third Republic in favor of what he considered to be, at the time, the only political force capable of unifying Europe against foreign incursions and reversing the trend of Western decadence that Nietzsche and Spengler had so lucidly analyzed. All in all, it goes without saying that 1934 was a primary turning point in Drieu's development as a political thinker and militant artist.

During the thirties, Drieu's talents as a novelist flourished in a most impressive fashion. After attempting a novel of manners with strong political overtones, *Une Femme à sa fenêtre (A Woman in the Window)*, 1929, he turned for inspiration to the tragic existence of his friend and former surrealist companion, Jacques Rigaut. In the novel, *Le Feu follet (Ghost Light)*, 1931, Drieu reconstructs the last two days in the life of Alain, a drug addict, within a framework of Racinian concision and purity. Just as Rigaut himself had done shortly before his suicide, Alain languishes in a rest home for wealthy neurotics in an unsuccessful effort to cure himself of his habit. Yet drug addiction is only a manifestation of a more profound social ill— that of decadence. As a child of the times, Alain has no reserve of self-discipline to draw upon. Appealing to his will power to overcome his difficulties, as the resident psychiatrist does, is a futile request. His friends cannot tolerate Alain's nihilistic despair which undermines their own sense of purpose and worth. Having spent his youth as an emotional and economic parasite, living off the generosity of his wealthy mistresses and estranged wife, Alain is now unable to endure the everyday pressures of life without the euphoric prophylaxis of drugs and easy money. His last gesture is one of total lucidity and resignation. He performs the only meaningful act he is still capable of accomplishing to lessen his anguish. He presses a revolver to his heart and pulls the trigger. Very few novels of this period have portrayed in such realistic terms the complete isolation of the individual in a world where even the most elementary communication is impossible. Ten years before the appearance of Camus' *The Stranger*, Drieu was examining, in *Ghost Light*, the problem of man's inability to touch others around him or find meaning in a world where he no longer seems to belong. Retrospectively, Alain can be seen as one of the precursors of the existentialist anti-hero: the social misfit whose existence is stripped of essential values and defined in the end only by an extreme form of action.

In 1933, one of Drieu's most personally revealing novels was published, *Drôle de voyage (Strange Journey)*. In much the same vein as *The Ladies' Man*, Drieu makes a romantic interlude in his own life the central focus of the work. While vacationing at the provincial home of a friend, Gille Gambier (Drieu's fictional counterpart), a young diplomat, becomes infatuated with a beautiful and wealthy Englishwoman, fleetingly contemplates marriage, but backs off at the last minute for fear of surrendering his freedom to the placid mediocrity of his fiancée's homelife. Disheartened by this experience, Gille resumes the "strange journey" of his affective odyssey, drifting from one casual affair to the next without being able to commit himself fully to another individual. In view of Drieu's use of literature as a means of self-awareness, the unsparing portrait he draws of Gille (i.e., his own reluctance toward any form of emotional involvement) tends to foreshadow the choice he will make the following year to escape the bondage of Parisian adultery and intrigue by devoting his life to a more exacting cause. This decision to forego dilettantism for political commitment was in part motivated by Drieu's horror of following in the footsteps of his father whose own life had been ruined by his sensual nature and lack of self-discipline.

Indeed, this obsessive concern with his youth and family background reaches its apogee in Drieu's next major novel, *Rêveuse bourgeoisie* (*Middle-Class Illusions*), 1937. As though compelled to do so after his father's death in 1934 (his mother had died in 1925), Drieu undertook the painful task of recasting his youth and early manhood into fictional form. By reliving in this manner his bitterly unhappy childhood, Drieu hoped to view his formative years in a clearer perspective as well as demonstrate, in the last analysis, that hereditary character flaws could be overcome by decisive action. Thus, in the military hospital where he lies dying of gangrene, Yves Le Pesnel knows that courage is the product of a willful act and that, by his heroism in combat, he had dispelled his fears of being contaminated by his father's weakness and failure in life.

Although heavily autobiographical in its conception, *Middle-Class Illusions* is nonetheless a thoroughly imaginative work of art in which, contrary to his narrative style, Drieu switches unexpectedly from a third-person to a first-person perspective in the final section of the novel. In so doing, Drieu chooses to continue the story of the Le Pesnel family from the point of view of Yves' sister, Genevieve—the only time in his writings that Drieu ever adopted a first-person female vantage point. In *Middle-Class Illusions*, Drieu temporarily suspends his misogynistic tendencies and portrays Genevieve in a favorable light. As an actress, she must artfully lie to her audience in order to give the illusion of reality just as the novelist must necessarily distort the past he seeks to recreate in his writings. By means of this male-female duality of narration, Drieu was trying to probe and elucidate a certain sexual ambivalence within himself that lay at the very heart of his negative attitude toward women. Overall, *Middle-Class Illusions* is an impressive cornerstone in the autobiographical edifice that Drieu constructed, book by book, in an effort to objectify his innermost conflicts.

Gilles (1939), by far Drieu's most ambitious work of fiction, is a prime example of how the autobiographical novel can become, through its treatment of the important literary and political issues of the times, much more than a reflection of the authorial self. Taking over in a sense where *Middle-Class Illusions* left off, *Gilles* recounts the sentimental and ideological odyssey of Gilles Gambier (a similar version of the protagonist in *Strange Journey*) from the trenches of the First World War to the bloody skirmishes of the Spanish Civil War. As a satirical work, *Gilles* cruelly lampoons the idiosyncracies and bold pretensions of the surrealist movement. For several years after the First World War, Drieu had been close friends with Louis Aragon and had actively participated in the group's demonstrations, especially the mock trial of Maurice Barrès. On a political level, the novel shows how certain conservative elements of the post-war generation in France (namely Drieu and other antidemocratic intellectuals) were attracted to fascism in protest over the ineptitude and venality of the scandal-ridden Third Republic. At the end of the novel, Gilles Gambier leaves the French diplomatic corps and casts his lot with the Franco loyalists in central Spain, thereby rallying to the fascist cause and renouncing the republican ideal in the process. In a similar manner, Drieu himself would publicly announce his intentions to collaborate with the German occupational forces in Paris shortly after the Fall of France. Thus, *Gilles* can be viewed not only as a critical summing-up of Drieu's life but also as a prophetic novel that foreshadows his entry into the collaborationist ranks.

In the articles written during the Occupation, Drieu tried to justify his collaborator's role by arguing that cooperation with the Germans was the only reasonable course of action open at the time to a conquered France. By accepting the German presence on their territory, the French could thereby hope to preserve their influence and position of authority in a unified Europe under German hegemony. In this regard, however, it is ironical to point out that even the German ambassador to France, Otto Abetz, had urged Drieu not to collaborate in an open manner, judging this to be an "unnecessary" risk.

Whatever Drieu's true motives may have been for collaborating with the enemy, it is certainly unjust—as Jean-Paul Sartre and other detractors have done—to accuse Drieu of cowardice or political expediency in this choice. Although he was offered asylum in neutral Switzerland before as well as after the Liberation of Paris, Drieu refused to leave his country, preferring to remain in spite of threats of reprisal by the French resistance movement. In view of Drieu's adherence to fascism as early as 1934 together with his membership in Jacques Doriot's Parti Populaire Français from 1936 to 1939 (the only well-established French fascist party), it seems obvious that any accusation of political opportunism on Drieu's part is wholly unfounded.

It should also be mentioned that, paradoxically enough, Drieu was an ardent patriot with strong nationalistic instincts, especially during the first days of the war when he offered his services to the French army but was turned down for health reasons. On the other hand, although little concrete evidence supports this assumption, it might well be that Drieu chose to collaborate with the Germans for basically suicidal motives—as Simone de Beauvoir and other critics have suggested. Sensing very early that Germany could not win the war, Drieu nonetheless reaffirmed his support of the occupational forces at every opportunity right up to the end. In so doing (as he confessed to his friend, Pierre Andreu, after rejoining Doriot's P.P.F. in 1942), he was aware that he would undoubtedly be executed by the *Résistance* once the Gemans had been driven out. Had he not taken his own life in March 1945, it stands to reason that Drieu would have been arrested, tried, and quite possibly condemned to death like his fellow collaborator, Robert Brasillach, who fell prey to the tide of vengeance that swept over France in the months following the Liberation. In light of Drieu's ideological intransigence and long history of partial suicide attempts, it does seem plausible that this ultimate desire to destroy himself may have been the deciding factor in his continued support of the Collaboration.

Despite the many crises and restrictions of the war years, Drieu experienced one of the most creative periods of his literary career. During this time, he wrote prolifically on a wide variety of subjects and in various genres. From 1940 until June 1943, Drieu also served as editor-in-chief of the prestigious literary magazine, *La Nouvelle Revue Française*—an appointment that raised a storm of controversy among its liberal, pro-Gaullist contributors. In 1941 one of Drieu's most impressive essays appeared, *Notes pour comprendre le siècle* (*Notes For Understanding Our Times*). This apology of totalitarian man and his ethos analyzes the progressive loss of equilibrium between mind and body from the Middle Ages to modern times. It was Drieu's contention that the totalitarian (primarily fascist) revolution of the previous two decades had been in truth a therapeutic correction of a profound social and spiritual malady, created by the excessive emphasis that Western societies placed on analytical skills to the detriment of intuitive or affective knowledge. By not developing his body on a parity with his intellect, twentieth-century man—prior to the advent of fascism—had burdened himself with a divided self which was the heritage of eighteenth-century rationalistic thought. At present, however, the totalitarian countries had restored the body and its imperatives to their rightful place by stressing the importance of sports and physical conditioning. In this manner, a new man—aggressive and vigorous—would arise and supplant his decadent predecessor of the rationalistic era. Together with a renewed physical dynamism, a sense of deep spiritual awareness would also reappear, fostered by the mystique of the new order. According to Drieu, therefore, fascism was primarily a restorative movement dedicated to purging Europe of its decadent spirit and introducing its people to an era of prolonged health—both politically and morally speaking.

As Drieu discovered shortly thereafter, Hitler's continental politics were unworthy of such encomiums. Progressively disillusioned over the imperialistic designs of the German armies and their disregard for the institution of a European confederation of national states, Drieu began to judge his political affinities and the Collaboration in a much harsher light. In 1943 Drieu published a novel of pivotal importance, *L'Homme à Cheval* (*The Man on Horseback*), which constitutes a symbolic farewell on his behalf to the concept of the heroic leader—or the fascist strongman—and a withdrawal from the political arena into an ascetic and contemplative existence. The second half of this essay will be devoted to an analysis of this novel and its relationship to Drieu's other works.

After this renunciation of political activism, Drieu next turned his attention to the Collaboration, its failure, and the question of individual guilt and responsibility in a France soon to be overrun by foreign armies. Although hardly one of Drieu's more polished novels, *Les Chiens de paille* (*Straw Dogs*), 1944, does manage to capture the spirit and critical issues of the times with bitter clarity. In this work, Drieu views the last throes of the Occupation through the eyes of a politically neutral observer, Constant Trubert, erstwhile soldier of fortune who finds himself in the service of a Parisian black market racketeer. A large cache of arms, hidden by patriots near the Brittany coast after the armistice between France and Germany, exerts a magnetic attraction on the rival factions of an occupied France. Gaullists, collaborators, fascists, right-wing nationalists, petty thieves and others all converge on the concealed treasure, hoping to claim it for their own causes. Although he becomes deeply involved in the conflicting intrigues, Trubert considers such maneuvering futile and prefers to meditate in the dunes or discuss painting and religion. Very similar to Drieu's own attitude at the time, Trubert's apathy derives from his belief that Frenchmen have lost all control over their personal and national destinies. They have all become sacrificial lambs for the foreign empires they represent in various surrogate capacities—in brief, they are "straw dogs" of no concern to those outside powers seeking total domination of Europe. Nonetheless, to give their lives a semblance of meaning, they go about stalking the hidden weapons with deadly seriousness. In the end, Trubert decides to sacrifice both himself and the others by blowing up the munitions storeroom, but a stray bomb, dropped by a British bomber and intended for a nearby factory, does the work instead—ironical proof that, in spite of everything, no Frenchman was free to dispose of himself as he saw fit.

For Drieu, the last days of the Occupation were, oddly enough, peaceful ones during which he slowly withdrew from life, preparing himself for the final ordeal. On August 12, 1944, as the Allied troops were approaching Paris, Drieu tried to kill himself but was saved at the last minute by his maid who returned unexpectedly to his apartment. After being transferred to the American hospital at Neuilly outside Paris, Drieu again tried to commit suicide by slashing his wrists but was rescued *in extremis* by one of the hospital staff. As soon as he had recovered, Drieu took refuge for the next seven months at several hideaways in and around Paris.

It was during this period of forced leisure that Drieu began to write again. In the brief essay, *Récit secret* (*Secret Tale*), he examines his own reasons for attempting suicide and explains how, even in childhood, this profound self-negation had played a constant role in his life. While in seclusion, he was also composing the first four sections of a novel partially inspired by the life of Vincent Van Gogh, *Mémories de Dirk Raspe.* For his final self-portrait, Drieu chose an unlikely model (or so it seems at first glance) in this tormented genius whose very sanity and life were ultimately sacrificed to his art. By selecting this fraternal spirit as the wellspring of his work, Drieu renewed the quest for a total self, but this time in the domain of visual beauty. The former channels leading to inner knowledge and unity— i.e., war, eroticism, and political commitment—were thus abandoned in favor of an ascetic devotion to art and religious meditation.

In January 1945, Drieu put aside his unfinished novel for good. The urge to destroy himself, as he explained in his diary, had come back very strongly. Two months later, after an extensive newspaper campaign calling attention to his case, a warrant was issued for Drieu's arrest. Unable therefore to leave his first wife's apartment in Paris where he was hiding, aware that he had very little time left before being arrested, Drieu finally succeeded in taking his own life by an overdose of barbiturates and gas inhalation. Next to his body a note was found, addressed to the maid who had saved him once before: "Gabrielle, let me sleep this time." Only a handful of close friends attended the funeral.

It is difficult to take the true measure of a controversial artist like Drieu without becoming embroiled in an ideological controversy that has little to do with his literary accomplishments. As a proponent of fascism—indeed, one of its outspoken advocates—Drieu has become in certain intellectual circles something of a "contaminated" writer. For reasons dictated by political antipathy and little else, his works are often downgraded or summarily excluded from serious consideration. While understandable on an emotional level—in view of the negative connotations of fascism—this attitude is not, however, critically valid when assessing the literary merit of Drieu's writings. Fortunately, as we stated earlier, hostilities have lessened with the advent of a new generation of critics, many of whom cannot remember the Occupation of France or even World War II itself. Since 1966 in particular, numerous articles and several book-length studies have appeared on Drieu. A widespread reappraisal of his writings is now under way among university scholars, although the majority of this criticism is being done outside France.

What is it, therefore, in Drieu's life and works that consistently attracts and sustains the interest of serious critics from a variety of national and political backgrounds? Other than the obvious narrative skills he possessed—Drieu was a first-rate storyteller as *The Man on Horseback* clearly demonstrates—it is most likely the intimate tone and almost painful candor of his observations that hold the greatest appeal for the contemporary reader. To be sure, as we mentioned at the first of this essay, no one who has carefully read Drieu can remain indifferent to his fictional presence. Even his bitterest enemies had to admit that, although misguided in his beliefs and political allegiance, Drieu was nonetheless an individual of integrity and complete sincerity. In the final analysis, it is mainly this quality of his work we most admire—the uncompromisingly honest investigation he pursued into himself as well as society at great personal expense.

Like other introspective novelists before him, Drieu firmly believed that the ultimate secret of existence could be discovered within the recesses of the creative mind. His obsessive probings and questioning, however, unearthed little more than partial imitations of himself but no total image as he had hoped. In the end, Drieu failed in the quest to unite the opposing facets of his personality. Yet, in more ways than we would perhaps care to admit, his troubled spirit strikes a responsive chord within us. In the dark mirror he held up to himself and his era, we can easily recognize our own anxieties and nostalgic yearning for a more cohesive and fulfilling life. Although modest in scope, Drieu's contributions to modern French literature are undeniably authentic and should be valued above all for the light they help to shed on the political and social crises that France experienced from 1917 to 1945.

Thomas M. Hines

PART I

DON BENITO'S CIGAR

I

Jaime Torrijos was a lieutenant in the Agreda cavalry regiment which was then stationed at Cochabamba. He was admired and loved by the officers and soldiers because there was exceptional strength and daring in his body. Women loved him for the same reason.

When I met him, his fame was beginning to spread beyond the regiment and the town. He enjoyed this in a carefree sort of way. I was a guitarist and became friendly with Jaime who wanted me at his orgies. He was always in need of money because of cards and women.

I was a guitar player but I had also been a seminarian. When I wasn't plucking my guitar, I was reading books on theology. I would observe men and women of all sorts and I saw how easy it was to influence them. The power that Jaime's valiant body exerted over men and women impressed me right away. Being a person who despised all power, I was curious as to whether this gift could be extended outside its native surroundings. Of course, the guitar was enough to make life a magical experience for me, yet I felt like introducing perilous forms into the innermost circle of myself.

During Jaime's orgies, I would observe him and improvise songs which vaunted his courage and that of the Agreda horsemen. They all fancied them and swelled with pride.

In those days, Benito Ramirez was Protector of the State. He was strong-handed and devious if need be, but his domination had lasted so long that his friends as well as his enemies were tired of it.

In my songs, I began to arouse contempt for the Protector and to threaten him with the disfavor of the Agreda horsemen. At first, I was only joking, but Jaime, who was bored and needed adventure and who had learned from me who he was, began to grasp the secret meaning of my songs.

One night, when he was drunk, he cried out: "Benito Ramirez stays in power because I let him."

The next day, I came into a woman's bedroom where he was and questioned him about this remark. He no longer remembered, but he soon agreed he had made it and even that he was aware of the motive behind his words.

It was then that he met Conception. Conception was the most beautiful whore in Bolivia and when she arrived in Cochabamba, Jaime only had eyes for her. She had been the mistress of many distinguished men in the capital and she despised the little lieutenant.

He wasn't as sure of himself with her as with the others and he solicited the privilege of her bed with a certain humility. He got his wish because he was strong and Conception could never turn down any powerful man and no one in the Agreda regiment would have wanted to stand in his way.

His strength pleased her.

As for me, I had been disturbed like everyone else by Conception's beauty and for a while I composed only those songs which vaunted the splendor of her breasts and hips and promised them to Jaime. After that, I praised their union and, finally, I became depressed and withdrew into theology.

It so happened, later on, that Don Benito Ramirez, coming from La Paz on his way to Santa Cruz, passed through Cochabamba. The Agreda regiment greeted him with honors in the plain at the gates of the city and were a marvelous sight to behold. I had come by mule to enjoy this display insomuch as, in spite of my frail constitution, I liked the beauty of men and horses. The powerful heaving of their chests caused my guitar to strum with the same fervor as did the breasts of beautiful women or the incredible ideas of theologians.

Ramirez sat awkwardly in his saddle. He was a small, round-shouldered man who carried his power with a sickly air. After the maneuver, he stopped in front of the regiment in battle formation and from afar I imagined the searching looks he must have given this unit whose recent mood had been reported to him by his spies. In the past, the Agreda regiment itself had supported his *coup d'état.*

Soon, he dismounted and sat wearily under a tree. I came closer and saw the regimental colonel, having been summoned, turn around and call Jaime. That made me a little anxious.

"Lieutenant Torrijos, I've been told that you don't like me," the Protector said in a calm, masculine voice—which was surprising from a mouth tormented by uncertainty. "It's possible that I was remiss in not recognizing your ability sooner. I'm promoting you to captain and assigning you to the dragoons in La Paz."

At first, Jaime seemed taken by surprise, but then he had never stopped peering into the Protector's eyes and finally he exclaimed: "I am grateful to you, Excellency, for making me a captain, but please do not give me a promotion if that means leaving the Agreda regiment."

"Captain, I gave you an order. You may go."

I admired the ease with which the Protector's beautiful voice moved through the air. That voice seemed to belong to a tall, quietly powerful man. I was in love with that voice and, that evening, at the officers' casino, I improvised a song on my guitar. I told of the sadness of an individual who reigns unchecked over others in order to assuage his contemptible rage and who is then amazed at their hate and constantly suffers from this.

Jaime was in a bad mood and was drinking a lot. Conception, who was nearby, was studying him with a mocking curiosity.

"Well, captain, you're finally going to meet the beautiful women of La Paz," she called out.

He no longer derived any pleasure from his power over other women since he had felt Conception's resistance. He was well aware that, in La Paz, he would be surrounded by spies and would probably be the victim of some ambush.

The officers were very upset by the announcement of their favorite's departure and were talking of nothing less than marching on La Paz during Ramirez's absence.

But then I quickly struck up a new song. The first words dumbfounded my audience. They told of Ramirez's strength and fame and of his justice. He had recognized the greatest captain in his army and had wanted to show him off to all the cavalrymen. Agreda would not forget Jaime Torrijos and soon the dragoons would love Torrijos just as Agreda loved him.

My listeners, at first displeased, finally understood my intentions, and on the last note there was a great uproar of laughter and applause.

A few days later, the captain joined his new unit and I too followed him into La Paz with Conception, whom we preferred to call

Conchita, and the old procuress who customarily regulated her disorderly life.

II

Now Jaime Torrijos was forced to plot against Ramirez. It was a question of life or death. While prodding my mule down the road, I had given a lot of thought to that instinct which pushes men to tempt fate and the strange understandings that exist between enemies. Without Ramirez's passionate concern, Jaime would possibly have remained an insignificant lieutenant in Cochabamba.

He was overwhelmed by the honor which had been bestowed on him. Knowing no fear, he was nonetheless extremely confused because he did not know how to deal with the situation.

I myself was a musician and was more contemptuous of procuring men for him than women—although I was ready to praise both on equal terms whenever men or women approached the object of my fancy. However, in the midst of dreams that flowed endlessly from my guitar at night, an idea came to mind.

At the seminary, I had known an unusual individual who was destined to become, as the French say, the *éminence grise* or power behind the throne. He was a professor of theology but was also involved in many other things.

I went to see him in his quarters which were always filled with little priests, whispering and snickering, whose servility he would belittle with a diabolical irony that all admired. He tossed about the most pretentious devices of scholasticism in a voice that any knowledgeable person would have eventually recognized as being deceitful. Yet, he was a former army officer who had entered the Church rather late in life.

I directed our chatter toward Ramirez's isolated position and I knew from Father Florida's wide stare, which casuistry had filled with burning flashes like coal-heated, white-hot irons, that some informant had already reported my relationship with Jaime to him.

"Don Ramirez is at an awkward age, for sure," he murmured while staring at the red edge of a large in-folio. A moment before, however, his eyes had wandered over my whole face like a somewhat abrasive caress.

"Well then, Father, who will aid the State?'

Afterwards, he took me out on the small balcony, covered with flowers, which was such a delightful contrast in his life to the unfurnished room at the seminary, decorated only by the distorted expressions that the priest knew how to elicit from his visitors.

"The colonel of the dragoons is the victim of a lone vice. This man, who neither drinks, nor eats, nor smokes, lives for his regiment, but unfortunately his enthusiasm extends even to his officers' wives."

Father Florida uttered this underhanded bit of news in a high-pitched, sing-song tone of voice while intently examining a large red flower and turning a distracted and exasperated profile toward me. I was so engrossed in contemplating this fallacious profile that he had to add, "... and to their mistresses."

Neither the colonel of the dragoons nor Conchita needed to be prodded into meeting each other. He had been promptly informed of the beautiful prize who was within reach and she in turn did not neglect this first opportunity to deceive Jaime—something she had not been able to do easily at Cochabamba, at least with someone who flattered her crude vanity.

Nonetheless, that woman was not thinking of leaving our captain. People were saying that he would be master of all Bolivia. She had little faith in this because she had never gotten over her first impression of having seen a little, inconsequential lieutenant; yet, an element of doubt kept her by his side as much as his virile presence.

At any rate, the colonel was very friendly to the new captain who didn't suspect a thing. As for me, I tried harder than ever before to get on the good side of Conchita.

One morning, I went into her bedroom together with the hairdresser. She was just coming awake and was displaying among the sheets a frightening collection of physical charms.

"Manuela, give me a cigarette!"

The old Indian woman slowly lighted a cigarette from the one she was puffing on between her sunken gums and gave it to her.

"My chocolate, Manuela. You're making me wait, you old hag, and I'm starving."

I played her a little tune to get her started off right. When she had finished drinking, she finally got up and turned herself over to her hairdresser who observed under her nightgown the very items that I didn't wish to see.

Suddenly, I began to play on my guitar the Agreda marching song about which I had often spoken with vociferous pride. She looked at me with astonishment and uncertainty. I winked and she fell into an apparent state of meditation, wrinkling her handsome forehead where normally a wrinkle-free, dazed beauty was in evidence.

When the hairdresser had left, she kicked Manuela out and we were alone.

"Conchita, you should be concerned about Jaime's life. The colonel has to tell you if Don Benito has said anything against Jaime to him."

She glanced furiously at me. Out of laziness, she thought her love affair had gone unnoticed.

"The colonel! Ugh! What influence do I have on the colonel? Stop talking about the colonel, you scoundrel!"

"The guitarist sees everything and says nothing. I don't want you to die."

"Bah! The captain loves me too much to kill me."

"He loves you too much *not* to kill you. But do you want the Protector to kill him?'

"No. Ramirez is ugly."

"Well then, we need the colonel on our side."

"Yes. Now go away."

The colonel was a wealthy nobleman and gave receptions at which Conception appeared as a dancer. I was her guitarist. Jaime was invited together with all the dragoon officers and soon the dragoons were like the Agreda cavalrymen—in love with Jaime and Conchita.

I anxiously wondered what Don Benito was thinking.

"What is he thinking?" I asked Father Florida.

"Everyone is conspiring. But one hundred small conspiracies do not make a major one."

"Perhaps."

"A major conspiracy, in the eyes of a Protector, is useful inasmuch as he can find in one group all those who are dangerous."

"We still have some time then."

"Perhaps."

III

I refuse to recount the political intrigue which brought things rather quickly to a climax, for political intrigue bores me, puts me to sleep. I sat playing the guitar in the midst of all the comings and goings, and music alone kept me awake. Sensing that violence was at hand, I had composed a chant which began with a very slow beat, swelled by fits and starts, each more surprising than the other, culminated in a frenzy of wild finger movements and receded into a sudden and doleful calm. This chant could well be our story.

I didn't pay much attention to his confederates, but at times I would observe Jaime Torrijos who, in a stimulating atmosphere, was growing like a beautiful, eyeless plant. He was stretching his arms toward the sun of his destiny with an admirable lack of awareness. Of course, he was unaware of all the complexities of his world, or so it seemed; nonetheless, his instinct kept me following his tracks and the sound of my guitar was like the promising glow of a talisman. In addition, without seeming to be involved, I would slip him a good piece of advice or perhaps loosen the tether of more than one troublesome detail.

It was strange that I would be confiding in this Father Florida whose eyes were so distant and, then, so close. But everything is an ambush and nothing ventured, nothing gained. Then too, we had common theological interests. Wasn't I his former pupil? Didn't we have the same dangerous curiosity about the Gospel of Saint John and the Apocalypse? For me, that was no guarantee at all but it made me prefer this juggler to anyone else—a person who would make knife-like thoughts dance in the air with feverish hands.

I had concluded then and there that he was very attracted in this respect to Torrijos and that he was not participating in our conspiracy only as Ramirez's spy. But why? Was he working like me to fulfill his own dreams or, on the other hand, was he obeying orders? He was a Jesuit but were Jesuits able to commit their minds to the lonely upheavals of this country hidden away in the mountains?

Typically, Jesuits are the ones who interfere in everything and even the most trifling matters.

Ramirez was the leader of the party behind which the privileged class of large landholders had taken shelter and he was their tool. Every tool, in the hands of those who use it, is rebellious and dangerous. So it was with my guitar itself which, even after years of practice, would often ignore my heart's pleas and desperate calling and give off a sound of studied indifference.

One evening, Don Benito showed up unexpectedly at the colonel's house just as all the officers had stopped drinking in order to watch Conchita dance.

"Gentlemen, excuse my indiscretion, but I was told that for some time the dragoons have known unusual pleasures which bring them together every night and I couldn't resist the urge to see for myself."

Always the beautiful, evenly modulated voice and that evil look which can neither satisfy nor replace the unattainable delights of a lost kindness.

Don Benito sat down, wet his lips indifferently with the drink set before him and motioned the dancer to continue. She was thrilled and danced superbly.

Our dances are always similar and never exhaust our emotional needs. They always tell the story of love that, although being a state of war between men and women, is also a state of war between men, excluding women. Conchita's body was voluptuous but loosened up at the sound of music as though it had not languished indolently all day long. It knew secrets that Conchita's heart as well as her mind were unaware of. In my case, being someone who despised all power and would have detested training the mind of the most gifted young man, filling him with ideas that I cherished on the coming of the Holy Spirit of whom Christ was only a precursor, I abandoned myself to the joy of shaping this innocent body that responded effortlessly to the specious rhythms of the song. At these moments, one has to believe that the universe is a single whole of which every vibration is communicated to all others with the most appealing complicity.

It was the heart of summer, in the month of January, and through the window I could see this glorious land of Bolivia rising up to the sky—so high that men exhaust themselves and only repeat with weariness and exasperation the acts of those down below.

Nevertheless, I didn't lose sight of Don Benito. He became very much a part of everyone's situation as if he had always been our companion—and in fact he had been as much through his spies. He was especially interested in Jaime Torrijos' expression as he watched Conchita dance and watched the men who were watching Conchita dance. The young captain's torture had begun the day he had met the beautiful woman. It was renewed at every occasion and that evening it was stronger than ever. For a moment Don Benito could rid himself of his own anguish by delighting in that of his rival and undoubtedly he had come just for this diversion.

Torrijos did not understand where those eyes were trained—eyes which nonetheless ignored Conchita's hips—and he thought that the Protector desired her. He could believe nothing else about any man. I sensed that henceforth his still vague ambition would give way to a much more active feeling in his heart—hate. That gave me a sense of satisfaction which was more surprising than anything I had yet experienced on his behalf.

I needed to express this satisfaction and while Conchita was resting, I struck up—with a daring that made a shiver run down my spine—the song of the Agreda horsemen which, for a short while, had been the song of the dragoons. I did not sing the words.

Don Benito's cold stare settled on me and I told myself that all was lost. I thought that I did not value my life but just then it seemed very sweet. I was bathed in my own perspiration out of fear. I needlessly congratulated myself for being so bold as to experience such emotions; nonetheless, that noble idea of risk went through my mind and that is all we can ask of our souls.

"Why don't you sing, guitarist? Come by tomorrow night and sing for me what you're keeping to yourself."

I acquiesced, more dead than alive.

IV

The next day, I had more or less recovered from the shock and I entered the governmental palace with a feeling of curiosity that dominated all the rest. It was here then that I had to bring Jaime. He had always lived in barracks and this one would be no worse than the others.

I had been told to come rather early in the evening, toward the end of dinner. I thought that I would have to wait or that I wouldn't get in at all or that some more unfortunate incident would occur, but nothing ever did, and all of a sudden I found myself in a large room full of books where the Protector, all alone, was smoking a cigar.

He hardly looked at me for a moment and then he spoke. He seemed to be straining to open his mouth and yet he managed to talk thereafter with the noblest of ease.

"Father Florida told me that you were plotting against me on behalf of Captain Torrijos."

It's too late now, I thought. Florida has betrayed us.

"I understand your idea to put this cavalryman in my place—he's handsome and I'm ugly. That idea is as good as another." I didn't know what to say.

"You can talk only when you have your guitar—well, get it."

"I left it in the waiting room."

"Go get it."

I did so, rather put out with myself. His beautiful yet stoical voice unnerved me. When I returned, I had calmed down somewhat—which was what Don Benito now seemed to want in a look filled with a strange goodness.

"Excellency, it is true that I only speak and think through my guitar and at Cochabamba, on uneventful days, a dreamy praise of Jaime Torrijos came from my guitar."

"So it seems. But what will he do—this Jaime who has seduced you or whom you've seduced—when he is ... Protector? Perhaps he'll choose, moreover, a new title."

"I don't know and I've never thought about it."

"So it seems. Bah! The government's ideas will come out of this guitar."

"Who knows? You might have acquired the idea of domination by listening to the wind blow in the mountains."

"No!"

He uttered this word so harshly that I thought the conversation would be over before it had actually begun. His armchair was located in a corner of the room in a special way so that a row of books was under his nose. Books which are not often seen in these parts. His look of somber and indifferent sensuality came from both his cigar and the books.

"So—you don't like politics," he continued after a long pause.

"Oh no, Excellency."

"So it seems."

He repeated these words with an ironical insistence. Once again he remained silent. The pretty blue twists of smoke matched the harmonious movements of his voice.

As I waited, forgetting my guitar, the position of the armchair forced me into an awkward posture, standing upright and a little to the rear. In order to see me, it would have been necessary for him to turn his head and upper body—something he did not do.

Suddenly, he said over his shoulder, "I'm not a politician. Circumstances have simply forced me to do what I've done."

Right then, I felt as though I were going to do something wrong, as though I were going to pay him a compliment.

"But since you control circumstances by thinking, your life takes on meaning."

He turned away but I had glimpsed a nervous tic.

"What kind?" he snickered.

"I'm beginning to think that you have a sense of duty."

"For a good guitarist, you're a bad poet, a conventional one. Circumstances have put me here and prevent me from leaving. That's all. But you're going to straighten out this mess with your Jaime."

Suddenly he stood up, threw his cigar on the floor and looked at me in an almost friendly manner. Then, he turned away and moved far from me to examine other books. While turning his back to me, he went on: "Ideas will come from the guitar and Father Florida will give them an acceptable form and Jaime will bang his fist on the table—on this table."

He went back to the table, lifted a large leather box and selected another cigar.

"But won't you stop all that?" I exclaimed, calling on him to help himself.

He gave me the same hard look that I had seen him give Torrijos.

"Perhaps. You may go now."

He hadn't offered me a cigar.

V

Upon leaving the palace, I was confused but not about the attitude the Protector might have. He hated us and would destroy us as soon as possible. He had sent for me in order to satisfy a passing fancy, above all to frighten us.

I was confused about the role Father Florida was playing. He had denounced us but, after all, he had told Don Benito only what the latter had already learned from his spies. That was perhaps merely a precaution.

I went to see Jaime and told him everything in detail. He listened with a thoughtful expression.

"He's tired and he's scared. You didn't get the point. He sent for you to open up negotiations. He thought you were more than a guitar player. But your inexperience served you well because there won't be any deal. We'll fight it out—as soon as possible."

Why was I more surprised by these words—that contained an error—than by those of Don Benito? I realized that until now I hadn't paid any attention to Jaime. For me he was a pebble I would throw into the water of my dreams and I was interested only in the ripples he would make. It didn't occur to me that if my ambitions had focused on him, it might well be for reasons other than his extraordinary demeanor. For several months he had been transforming himself as well as others.

"I don't think for a minute, Jaime, that Don Benito wanted to negotiate with me. He knew I was nothing more to you than a humble friend."

I stopped, deciding it was impossible to explain to Jaime that Don Benito was a dual personality, both contemplative and active, and that he had needed me to test his monologue on himself, but that this misjudgment did nothing to lessen his combative determination.

"Well then, why would he have wasted his time?" Jaime scoffed. "He doesn't like music and you told me he didn't make you play."

"But where does Father Florida fit in?" I asked, not without some anxiety.

"He's playing both sides. He can't do otherwise and we'll ask nothing more of him than to betray us in the same way he's betraying Ramirez. It's his way of taking an interest in people."

Yes, Jaime was much shrewder than he seemed. I was surprised to find that he possessed, after all, those attributes I had imagined he would have.

A few nights later, as I was going to the café El Dorado, a little boy grabbed me by the legs and said, "Follow me."

He began to walk toward a rather suspicious-looking small street. I said to myself, "This is one of Don Benito's ambushes. I don't have long to live." I ignored him and continued on my way.

The next day, I received a note from Father Florida who complained about not seeing me any more and urged me to come visit him. I hurried over, full of curiosity, but a stranger stopped me very near the seminary and suggested that I come with him into a garden, the door of which was partially open. He didn't look like a cop but was well-dressed, rather stout, and seemed to be an intelligent person. I took a chance, although I was hardly pleased at how small his arms were.

He walked among the quincunx for a moment without saying a word, studying me boldly. Then he spoke his mind: "My friends and I are very interested in Captain Torrijos. He is a noble and courageous man."

He looked at me in a knowing way as though I were supposed to understand what he was hinting at. I was baffled.

"Captain Torrijos could bring back into Bolivian politics those feelings of nobility which made Bolivar and Sucre great."

"Excuse me, sir, may I ask your name?"

"Whether it's Fernandez or Gonzales doesn't matter. What counts are the ideas that we are promoting. Therefore, let Captain Torrijos know that important men, who can weigh heavily in his favor, are following his undertaking with the sincerest interest. Tell him that we are ready to help him in every way possible."

"But really, sir—"

"Really what? Don't you understand that we completely disavow Ramirez's tyranny and we want to return to republican government, to government by the people."

"But the people have never governed."

"The indeterminate will of the people can be represented by a group of enlightened, reasonable individuals, each of whom respects the dignity of man in others and does not attempt to surpass them and force upon them a power seized by deceit and violence."

"That's aristocracy."

"No, that is democracy."

"Our people are made up of poor, deprived Indians who cannot delegate any power or ideas to their representatives, as you say. The representatives don't represent anything except themselves."

"Not at all. They represent secret forces which are entirely real."

This fat man looked at me more seriously than ever before. He raised a dialectical forefinger—"Let us consider for a moment the present situation. Strictly speaking, Don Benito is a tyrant, isn't he?"

"Yes."

"Do you want to remove him?"

"Yes."

"Is it, therefore, for the purpose of overthrowing tyranny?"

I was going to cry out so naively—no! in order to put a new tyrant in his place! And for a while, I would have unfurled all the simple cynicism of my thinking which was to believe that no system has ever existed except that of every man for himself. But I realized all of a sudden that such things were not said when one wanted to succeed in politics and that the rules of that game had to be followed in order to win. A cheat doesn't operate in the open; otherwise, the other cheaters begin to howl.

I gave my worthy interlocutor a sugary look.

"Your reasoning, sir, is inevitable. It is indeed a fact that if we want to overthrow a tyrant, it is because we are opposed to tyranny itself."

"Ah, very good. I knew that you couldn't talk any other way. A friend of the noble Torrijos can only be a friend of freedom. We can then come to an agreement and I will carry back to my friends the most favorable impressions."

"Your friends?"

"You shall meet them. It will be an honor for us to have you as a guest and I am certain that you will not regret adding our knowledge to that which you have been able to acquire yourself through reading, meditation and experience concerning the meaning of the world. Meanwhile, please inform the captain of our favorable inclination."

He bowed ceremoniously. I did the same and we went back to the garden gate. Just as I was about to go out, he caught me by the sleeve.

"Please believe that I am not indifferent to the pertinence of your remarks on the problems of democracy. You seem to favor aristocracy. In that respect we may well be in agreement with you and much more fully than you think. Yet, what matters is that aristocracy be enlightened. Enlightened—that's the secret... And should the captain need ... immediate help, don't hesitate to let us know."

Back in the street, I smiled and even laughed in a very relaxed manner. Not only were the Jesuits, by way of Father Florida, taking an interest in our Jaime, but so were the Freemasons. An ambitious person is not by himself for long in this world.

I was anxious to compare the words I had just heard with Father Florida's comments. I was only a short distance from his quarters. Just as I was going through the door, I saw him leaning over the railing of the small, flower-strewn terrace. He had possibly seen me encounter the stranger at the end of the street.

When I had paid him my respects, he chased away from the terrace those little priests who had dared venture forth and, having darted his pupils at me, he searched for some flower to inspect. Once he had singled out the thick, full petals of a magnolia blossom, he then casually remarked, "Doctor Belmez is a very discreet man."

"Ah, was that Doctor Belmez who stopped me at your door?"

"It's rather typical of things today that, while going to see a Jesuit, one encounters a Freemason. Doctor Belmez is well versed in the cabala and in the past I had some rather stimulating discussions with him when I was in the army. He was a surgeon then."

I had heard about Doctor Belmez. I should have known about or recognized him.

"Doctor Belmez got out of the army after marrying one of the Bustamente sisters. He is very well off."

For a moment I was lost in thought and he let me speculate about this Bustamente family, famous for the beauty of its daughters.

"Well, Father, I had the honor of visiting briefly with Don Benito who told me that you had spoken to him about me."

"La Paz is a very small town where everything is known. It is useless to hide anything."

"I agree completely."

"Everything is known—that is a manner of speaking, because one doesn't know what are the true thoughts of Captain Torrijos."

"That's what I've been telling myself recently. Possibly, Father, you know more about this than I do, but I am not asking you any questions."

"A moderate amount of discretion is required, my child. The Church exercises this virtue in a superior manner with respect to all things which transpire in this century."

"But it is concerned, nonetheless, with the innermost regulation of contemporary affairs."

" 'Innermost' is a well-chosen word."

"You get along quite well with the Freemasons in these innermost circles."

"Oh yes, but one should not trust superficial comparisons."

"Of course. That's why I wonder if you are putting Ramirez and Torrijos on an equal footing."

"That remains to be seen."

Father Florida had given in to the temptation and plucked a magnolia blossom petal that he first stroked with a single finger, then slowly crumpled with ten cruel and unrestrained fingers. He only discussed subtle trivialities with me for the rest of my visit.

VI

One night, at eleven o'clock, Conchita had me come to the colonel's house. Not without a trace of astonishment, I found gathered together—in addition to the colonel—Jaime, Father Florida, and an infantry captain that I had not met.

Jaime said to me, "Felipe, our priest wanted you to be here."

Father Florida cast one of his brief and penetrating looks at Jaime, then smiled casually at me.

"Colonel, we can't wait any longer," Jaime exclaimed. "We must, next Monday, attack the palace and shoot Ramirez."

The colonel was a powerfully built old man with a florid complexion and pink hair who struggled mightily not to stare every second at Conchita who was wearing a dangerously low-cut gown. He let out a terrifying groan.

"No longer wait?! But ever since you arrived a month ago, you've upset my troops, who no longer obey me, and now you want to involve us in a wild scheme whose outcome is uncertain."

The colonel stared blankly straight ahead at this uncertain outcome. Then, he turned toward Father Florida who was also gazing at Conchita's shoulders, but with an icy curiosity.

"Father, can you predict the outcome of this venture?"

"Certainly, colonel. In Bolivia the dragoons are going to bring back moderate government which never should have been insulted as it has been over and over for twenty years. Don't you have the greatest respect for the tradition of Bolivar?"

The colonel felt justified in calling upon Conchita and the magnificent expanse of her body as witnesses of his reverence for Bolivar.

Jaime turned toward the infantry captain who was slim, vigorous and quiet.

"Captain Fernandez can vouch for two-thirds of his unit."

The captain feverishly added, "Soldiers, not officers, and we will have to arrest the colonel. But it's entirely possible."

The captain bared his teeth. He was delighted at the pro-aspect of arresting his colonel—a raw delight that made bile flow in his veins.

"Well then, we're going to draw up a plan of attack. Give me some paper."

But there was no paper in the house. Father Florida took out a small notebook from which he tore two or three sheets with a sigh.

Jaime began to draw, pressing down so hard with his pencil that the paper gave way and the future operation looked like fly droppings.

I watched with resignation as Father Florida intently followed Jaime's demonstration. Tomorrow he would report everything to Don Benito. What would happen then? This was all getting serious—we were going to our deaths. Consumed with a desire to live, I asked myself if we shouldn't assassinate Father Florida at the end of this meeting. What indeed did Jaime think?

He was so long in explaining matters to the colonel and the captain that Conchita, tired of smoking and drinking, asked me to get my guitar.

Jaime cursed to make her be quiet but finally he ended his recommendations that revealed the most elementary daring—that is, a complete understanding which seemed to charm Florida.

"Captain, I would have enjoyed having you as one of my students. You would have done remarkably well in logic."

"I'm afraid of books," Jaime murmured. "Sing now, Conchita."

Conchita and I took turns playing and singing. Then she had to dance. To stifle her boredom she had been drinking a lot. As a result, she gyrated with a lasciviousness that went beyond the limits of common decency. The colonel had also been drinking and could no longer contain his delight. Jaime began to study him—mighty colonel that he was—like an ox ready for slaughter and whose noose was being measured.

During a break, I took Jaime aside.

"Jaime, Father Florida will turn your plans over to Don Benito tomorrow."

"No, idiot."

"He kept him informed of our very first steps."

"So as not to show him what was coming next."

"How do you know?"

"Father Florida knows that Don Benito can't last. For him, I'll do as well as anyone else."

"But these Jesuits are interested in keeping Ramirez who belongs to the major landholders."

"They think that change is inevitable."

"You've become very perceptive, Jaime."

"Like Conchita, you think I'm stupid because I'm good-looking. You like me and you also despise me."

I was amazed at the extraordinary growth of our Jaime. "What about Dr. Belmez? If the Jesuits come over to our side, the Freemasons will be against us."

"No. I've seen Belmez. I've reassured him."

"And the Jesuits as well?"

"Them too."

"This is all very confusing."

"Both groups have never done more than witness events."

"At any rate, Father Florida will decide our fate tomorrow."

"I've told you, idiot, that if I weren't around, then someone else would rise up against Ramirez."

VII

The following night, having played at the El Dorado café for an unappreciative audience, I was sadly making my way home when the raucous sound of galloping horses shook my humble street. It was Jaime, followed by several dragoons. He stopped in front of my door.

"Felipe, jump on this horse and follow me!"

By the two breasts of the Virgin! He had Conception across his saddle and she was bound and gagged.

I didn't jump on the horse—I dragged myself on—and after that I had to hold on with great difficulty. Our party traveled through back streets to reach the outskirts of town. We were soon in the country where galloping seemed to be less dangerous than on our capital's pointed cobblestones.

But, since our pace did not let up, my buttocks were soon afire, my back was aching and my heart was beating wildly.

I took advantage of a sort of rest stop at a road crossing to seek out Jaime.

"Ah, you've got your guitar. I was afraid you had left it behind."

I realized, as a matter of fact, that I had tied it to my belt with my handkerchief and that it wasn't broken.

"What's going on?"

"I'll tell you later."

"Where are we going?"

"To Cochabamba to join up with the troops from Agreda."

I won't recount the trip which for me was torturous because we went without stopping at breakneck speed. Once we arrived, sleep prevailed over curiosity. When I inquired about Jaime, I was walking like a duck, with my buttocks all aflame.

Jaime laughed when he saw me. I asked him some questions but I had to work at deciphering his laconic answers in order to understand what had happened. Jaime had grown jealous of the dragoon colonel and had put him under surveillance the following day. In that manner, he had been able to surprise him toward evening in a suburban house where he was entertaining Conchita. He had killed the colonel, kidnapped the girl and decided to join forces with Agreda.

I sighed deeply—we were lost.

"What can we do?"

"What can we do? Don't you hear the trumpets? In an hour, we're going to march on La Paz."

With that, he turned away. I asked all around, trying to find out what his battle plan might be. I was told that some of the garrison at La Paz had been encouraged to revolt by Fernandez after we had left and they were waiting outside the city for us to reinforce them. With the other army units dispersed to all parts of the country, we would probably be able to fight on equal terms in the vicinity of La Paz.

What about Conchita? What had happened to her? It was rumored that Jaime had locked her up somewhere, if he hadn't already chosen the worst possible fate for her. I prayed to the Madonna that this might be true. After all, the Madonna is perhaps not as indulgent with whores as was her Son.

As best I could, I sat my raw posterior on the back of a mule and took my place at the tail end of the regiment. As we were setting out, Jaime had gone to the head of the troops with a magnificent bearing that had evoked unanimous applause from soldiers and officers alike. Those from Agreda thought that Jaime had played a good trick on the dragoons and that the colonel's shameless audacity was reason enough for administering a good saber thrashing across the backs of all that brood.

If my buttocks hadn't hurt so much, I would have been completely happy with our expedition. Nothing is more beautiful than to walk at night in our country. We live at thousands of feet above sea level, and no matter where one looks, there are always, near or far away, even higher mountains. The heart grows heavy when one thinks that, carried so high, man is not master of a different fate than in Peru or Chile, the lowest countries of all. The moonlight was so pure that one had the impression of not being on earth but far up in the sky, in some more secure center of the universe. The mountains, covered with indestructible snows, were milky ways very close to my soul. Beyond the clanging and rumbling of the column, I perceived a more penetrating silence than that in my books. O theologians, you do not realize that you are also poets and that you haunt the same eternal peaks where, in the beauty of the night, exalted lyrical poetry comes to fulfill your basic stammerings!

From the horses and men there rose a strong odor which blended the most courageous alacrities of the earth with my celestial happiness. Now that my buttocks had grown accustomed to their perpetual bruising and since I had been thrust toward my destiny again by this manly smell, I could picture myself as the centaur Chiron who educated Hercules to the strains of a lyre. From time to time, whenever an elevation in the road made it possible, I would see my Hercules, looming tall ahead of the men and horses.

A little later, I couldn't stand it. Kicking the sides of my much too peaceful mount, I moved toward the head of the column until I reached our leader. I offered the usual excuse of my daring ways and laid my guitar on the pommel of my saddle.

"That's it, Felipe, sing—sing of tomorrow's victory."

In a voice I had never known before, I broke into the song of the Agreda horsemen. At that moment, it seemed as though all the animality we were carrying behind us awakened to the incredible beauty of the location. Horses stretched their necks, shook their silver curb chains and two or three neighed. At the refrain, the men's souls were lifted in a single thrust above their bodies swaying on their mounts. The highest choir on earth created the magnificent illusion of a song that reached right up to the stars.

Ah, if you haven't heard the full-throated singing of men who, by the grace of war, know at last that they will be facing death every day, you cannot know the fleeting beauty of being their brother. This takes place when horses are preferred to women and steel to gold.

Blessed be Apollo and the sun god of the Incas, for I have celebrated men more often than women. Moreover, in our regions of Indian ancestry, women admire men and expect nothing else but their charitable scorn.

When we were tired of singing, I asked Jaime, "What have you done with Conchita?"

"I whipped her. I'll be victorious before she's well again." In the dark, his voice was steady and I said to myself that the call of battle had torn him away from the hapless appeal of the dancer who wasn't aware that his steps were entering the pathway of the stars over our heads. I was bitterly happy that she was far away and I thought I recognized the same wild satisfaction in my master's voice, from the shadow of his hat.

"What will you do when you're victorious, Jaime?"

I have always regretted such a question at that moment.

"Bah!" Jaime growled. "Keep singing."

"No. It wouldn't be the same."

VIII

When the fighting began, I was completely infused with pride but it was a pride I wanted to share with all my comrades and which must be called love. Excited by the approach of a totally unknown event, yet which right away seemed designed to fill my heart, I had slipped into a scouting detachment. I was still perched on my mule and I didn't have a saber, only a pistol. We were on a small road, boxed in between two high banks, that went down into a hollow and then rose up opposite us until it reached a ridge over which it disappeared. Suddenly, we saw several enemy horsemen appear on that ridge. They were wearing a red armband whereas we had a white armband. In our country, the red party was the party of the nobles and the white party, the democratic party, contrary to Europe. May I say that before a thought had time to cross my mind, I had already taken my dagger from my boot and plunged it into the rump of my mount that brayed wretchedly and, after two or three lunges which should have pitched me to the ground, carried me forward. Our men leaped into action and, riding more warlike creatures, overtook me in a flash, heading straight for the approaching troops.

In the hollow of the road, there was a skirmish and, thanks to my dagger, I wasn't too late in getting there.

My frenzied mule, by its bucking, undertook to assure me an unusual role in the fray. So violently indeed did the two of us crash into friend and foe alike that we were finally knocked to the ground. The fall seemed rather long but the contact with the gravel was harsh and lacerating, and I lost somewhat that blessed sense of terrestrial matters which I was then enjoying.

When I came to, there were no more than two or three bodies like me lying in the road. My right arm and leg were very painful. My clothes were torn and I was bleeding. My mule had gotten up and, forgetful of its indignation, was grazing upon some brush. I stood up as well, but not without feeling some rather sharp pain. A man on the ground was cursing me. He was a "Red" and he demanded water from me as though it were his right.

At that moment, I turned around and I saw our men disappear in the direction we had come from. I told myself that the others who had completely withdrawn beyond the ridge were going to return in force and I ran after my mule. But it would have nothing to do with me and, by its gambols, let me know that it was not interested in carrying such a fierce warrior. I decided to go on foot but my wounds became irritated and my right thigh was of little use to me. As I limped back up the high-banked road, I often looked anxiously behind me.

My intuition was correct because a much larger group of enemy horsemen came into view and began to rush down toward me. If I stayed on the high-banked road, I would be overrun in a second by their charge. I hastily started to climb one of the banks. It was very steep and gave me a lot of trouble because of the numbness of my limbs on my right side. The loose stones gave way under my boots and clutching hands and, after a first attempt, I tumbled back down. I immediately started up again, out of breath and groaning; however, when the charging horses arrived, I hadn't lifted myself completely out of reach and a saber blow, by chance poorly administered, ripped open my leather trousers at the very spot where they had already been badly scuffed by my fall.

A horseman who was a little to the rear of the group spotted me and, as I got to the top of the embankment, I saw him unhook his musket from his saddle. I still had my pistol.

I cocked it and shot at him, but the shot didn't go off. I turned around to run. But the top of the embankment on which I was crouching on all fours formed a narrow balcony beyond which the terrain began to climb very sharply. I saw a large rock toward which, having stood up, I retreated—but backwards, since I didn't dare lose sight of my tormentor. My heels struck some stones and I fell over backwards. That is what saved me, for the man had trained his weapon on me and his bullet whistled overhead.

He swore like a madman but his horse moved violently to one side and, suddenly changing his mind, he deserted me and galloped away to rejoin his companions. I found myself sitting down, seized by a violent fit of trembling. In order to regain some of my composure, I took a few coca balls that I had in my pocket. Noting that the embankment on the other side of the road was not nearly so high and disappeared into a rather thick underbrush, I decided to cross over to the other side of the road which was deserted and that was soon done, but not without more scratches. I crawled for a long time in the underbrush and finally found myself on a footpath where I could stand up.

Just then, I recovered a small measure of the plenitude of my consciousness—no longer being concerned with my physical survival alone. I noticed that on all sides there was heavy firing, that the battle was under way and that Jaime's future was at stake. Where was he? An agonizing curiosity urged me to find him as soon as possible. But how? I could see nothing but underbrush from where I was standing. I moved briskly along the footpath on the uphill slope in hopes of reaching some sort of lookout. I walked for a long time without success, but finally I found an old tree struck by lightning. I was able to hoist myself a little on its rotten trunk and I saw again, down below, the accursed road where I had first tasted combat. I mentioned before that, rising and falling, it crossed a valley. The embankment I had first scaled prevented me from seeing the depth of this valley in front of me, which continued to widen until it reached a village. At this point, there was heavy fighting and I saw puffs of smoke streaked with flashes of light. I had to return then to the ill-fated road, cross over it again and approach the village by way of the valley. There I would get a good idea of what was happening.

I stumbled down the path and arrived at the road. It was still deserted. As I crossed it, I saw my mule which was still there among the wounded. I called to it but it turned away after studying me with a snide expression. I slowly went up to it, so slowly that, like a fool, it let itself be caught and mounted without too much resistance. As soon as I had become its master again, I felt better situated and I started out down the valley toward the village.

As I came closer to the thundering struggle, I was more appreciative of the tranquillity of this off-stage area where I contemplated stopping for a while. A stream flowed near the path and it would have been sanitary to bathe my wounds in its waters, yet the current's murmuring sweetness did not persuade me. To me it seemed a state of mind as vain as a theologian's remark on worldly indifference.

When I got near the village, I reappraised my situation— I must not fall into the enemy's hands. I got off my mule, tied it up securely, and reloaded my pistol. I edged forward through a corn field until I reached the first house. This was not the area where the fighting was going on. Hearing very little noise, I went inside. I discovered some women and children who started to scream. It was impossible to get the slightest explanation. I then went down a sort of alleyway at the end of which I heard some noise without seeing anything.

Afraid that I would unexpectedly come across an enemy unit, I moved forward very hesitantly. Looking up, I saw—above the squalid houses—as pretty a church tower as can be seen in our countryside. I gazed at it for a moment against the sky. Then, I continued to move cautiously forward. Suddenly, a noise made me turn around. Two men rushed at me and seized me. They were wearing a red armband. Although I had taken off my white armband, they seemed to know whom they were dealing with because they hastily dragged me off.

A minute later, I was pushed into the village church, and was enjoined with rifle butts to climb the steps to the bell tower. With pounding heart, I imagined that they were making me climb to the top only to push me off. At the top, I found myself face to face with

Don Benito who, almost by himself, was sitting at an embrasure and studying the battlefield as he smoked a cigar.

That man had the unfortunate habit of not looking at me. But he had undoubtedly seen me in the alleyway, from on top of his observation post, with my face turned up.

"Is that you—the guitarist?" he asked, with no more than a glance in my direction.

"Yes, Excellency," I answered in a choked voice.

He gave a signal and my abductors removed their heavy claws from my aching shoulders.

There were two or three officers who were standing at the other openings of the bell tower. Don Benito was looking out and from a distance I could also see over his shoulder. At first it was difficult to understand through the smoke rising toward us. I could see vague lines of soldiers here and there, outside the village—scanty formations which were advancing or wildly firing away. I was too far from the embrasure to see what was happening in the village itself. But a short while later the shooting and commotion seemed to move away from us.

"Your stupid friend is getting beaten."

Once again I was under the spell of his manly and calm voice. I was also engulfed by the feeling of no longer being in danger. I took two steps toward the embrasure.

Without turning around, Don Benito blurted out, "Here's where he's losing ground. That's my center. He's thrown almost all his infantry units against this center and they're being destroyed."

A loud noise in the stairway—a messenger came in. The man had a powder-blackened face on which sweat was tracing a mobile tattoo. The officers gathered around him.

"Excellency, they're moving back."

His Excellency did not answer and his face in profile remained distracted. Here was someone who loved cigars more perhaps than anything else in the world.

The messenger, catching his breath, gave me a ferocious look. I wondered if Jaime's entire operation was not going up in smoke. What had I been dreaming of?

Don Benito gave orders to the messenger and the two officers. The one who was left found my presence offensive.

"What's to be done with this man, Excellency?"

"Nothing. Leave him here ... Well now, this is interesting." Don Benito took his spy glass and looked off in the distance. His voice had broken slightly. I moved closer and looked over his shoulder. Far away, a cavalry unit was approaching the village in a deployed formation. I guessed that this was Jaime's cavalry, the Agreda regiment. I was ashamed of having let myself be captured so easily. It seemed that, in this enemy observation post, I was like a traitor to my friends. I looked toward the stairway. Wasn't there some way to slip away? But the two soldiers who had brought me here were still there and there were others below.

"Very good," Don Benito said.

I watched and suddenly I understood. The Agreda horsemen were advancing at a trot on an unprotected stretch of ground leading right up to the entrance to the village. But a slight rise in the terrain on their right prevented them from deploying in that direction. It so happened that foot soldiers with red armbands were hiding on the other side of this land fold—in such a way that the troopers were going to be outflanked by the government soldiers' fire at the very moment they would come up against the first houses in the village. At that point, the gradually decreasing gunfire was most likely indicative of the fact that Don Benito's supporters had won out.

It seemed as though Jaime, whom I could now make out at the head of Agreda, was going straight to his death. Sweat ran down my body. It was then that Don Benito turned around and studied me with an expression of restrained malevolence.

"Do you see now?"

"It's not over yet."

He turned back to his enemy.

The Agreda horsemen began to gallop. Ah! Agreda, how beautiful you were and I was not with you. Fate, with its derisive sense of justice, had brought me back to my contemplative nature. I was suffering. I looked behind me. The soldiers had rushed to the bell tower's embrasures and the stairway was unguarded. But, too late, for the sight of the action was gripping.

I had often seen Agreda drilling and parading and now I was seeing it at work in the magnificently succinct abbreviation of its boasting and vanity, of its pride and love. It was one of those unusual moments when man has the opportunity to be himself by propelling himself completely beyond himself. It was one of those moments when men are truly friends and are dissolved into a love that haughtily exceeds all love. Men and horses, at the height of their animalistic spirit, became centaurs that rushed in a semi-divine charge toward our bell tower—whose bells should have been ringing. O magnificent row of chests which were heading toward us, which were climbing toward us! O flowing manes! O tails! O froth! O long, useless cry! O mystery of mankind which gives itself for nothing to nothing! O frenetically self-sufficient beauty! O minute forever lost, forever eternal in the heart!

My chest was pressed against Don Benito's back who continued to smoke his cigar and was not worried any more than I about the possibility of a hand pushing him from the bell tower to punish him for what was going to happen ... and which did happen. Don Benito's infantry stood up all along the knoll on Agreda's flank. A terrifying enfilade fire created confusion in the squadron on the right. The horses collapsed, reared up, fell back on top of each other. The centaurs were disintegrating, soul to one side, body to the other. I saw Jaime turn his head toward the misfortune, then face to the front again and lift his saber. Agreda kept on advancing, and grew enormously visible in every frantic detail.

Then, there were three loud explosions at the edge of the village. Don Benito had placed a battery there. To the right and left of Jaime, behind him, there were two holes in the wave of his men.

The troopers were coming close to the village. They were lost in the smoke from musket fire which was coming from there. How many of them were left? Jaime would surely be killed. I could see nothing else and that made me think of escaping again. I turned around and the stairway was there, gaping wide. Don Benito and the others were scarcely thinking about me. I backed away step by step and dashed into the stairway.

IX

How I got out of the village, found a horse and headed for safety is something I won't recount because I was tired of shuffling around on the sidelines and I did what was necessary in a murky haste. I had torn myself away in horror from the lure of Don Benito and the lure of contemplation. I wanted to find my companions again and share their defeat and grief and I especially wanted to find Jaime again, dead or alive. I was so indifferent to all the obstacles I might encounter that I overcame them without hindrance in the dream of my desire. The combat zone was narrow and, making a rather wide detour, I found myself very soon after at the rear of Jaime's small army.

As it was easy to predict, the attack on the village had failed and turned out to be a bloody defeat. Small groups of soldiers, exhausted and blood-stained, flowed back around me. I asked everyone where Jaime could be. Some answered that he was dead, others cursed him and myself as well, others shook their heads without saying anything. The sound of fighting had progressively ceased and only intermittent gunfire was heard which told me where our rear guard units were located. If Jaime were still alive, that is where he would be. I spurred my horse in that direction.

Jaime! Coming around a curve in the road, I saw Jaime. He was riding alone, at the head of a small group of Agreda cavalrymen. I went toward him and my heart writhed with despair at the thought that he was going to suspect something about my foolish escapade and doubt my loyalty, if not my courage.

He watched me coming with indifference, then his face brightened somewhat—I had forgotten that I was covered with blood and my clothes were torn.

"Well, guitarist, you fought too. That's good."

My heart fluttered with relief and turning my horse about rather cavalierly, I came up alongside Jaime, boot to boot.

"It's all over, guitarist."

"No, Jaime."

"I've killed enough men already as it is. It takes more than courage."

"War can change directions in a second."

"Be quiet."

We rode for a while without speaking. But this silence was a terrible burden for me and I was certain that his fate was in my hands. Night was falling and I viewed the shadows with bewilderment, like a poor theology student to whom an examiner has just put a very difficult question and who, at first, feels nothing but the blankness of his mind. I had to come up with something. Over and over, I saw nothing but Don Benito's back at the embrasure of the bell tower and the smoke of his cigar. That gave me an idea.

I suddenly stopped my horse and shouted, "Stop, Jaime!"

"What?" he roared in a sudden fury.

"We have to go back."

"Idiot!"

"No, they've stopped fighting. They're not following us. They won't be on their guard. I know the way and I'll lead you to where Don Benito is and we'll take him by surprise."

He answered me with a stream of curses and moved his horse along the road of retreat. I returned to his side and pleaded with him for a long time. My explanations finally seemed strange to him and he shouted at me, "You're a traitor! You want to lead me into a trap! Arrest him!" he shouted behind him.

An officer came toward me, his pistol raised high.

"Jaime, I'm offering you your last chance. If you kill me, then you might as well kill yourself."

"Wait," he said to the officer. "Dismount."

We all got off our horses.

"Let me tell you about it, Jaime, and you'll understand."

"Anybody still got a cigar?"

A man handed him a shapeless fragment in such a tender way that I regained confidence in our destiny.

"Come with me and talk."

He led me to one side. During my story, he looked at me first with an incredulous and suspicious expression, then a sort of gleam came to his eyes. He was perhaps more astonished to discover a soul so different from his own than to glimpse the incredible perspective that I was showing him. I furnished him with a specific plan. I ended with these words: "If you have to die, it's better to die like this. And the men who are here also prefer to die while playing their last card rather than hiding under the table."

I saw Jaime suddenly come alive. The challenge was winning him over. He explained everything to our men who, in the dark, were flabbergasted. The leader's speech was followed by a long murmur.

"If we continue to retreat, we'll lose everything. If we carry it off, La Paz is ours."

I had said that in a voice that I didn't know I had.

"And if you betray us, I'll cut your guts out with this knife," someone said.

"Yes, that's right!"

"Let's eat, drink and leave," Jaime decided.

One more ride that I won't describe. And yet, whereas the previous one had taken place, as I said, in a split second because of the dullness of my senses which were receptive only to essential impressions from outside, now, while I was guiding Jaime and his small band, I was in a completely different state of mind and the sudden lack of interest I showed in the unique and primary objective of our quest made me susceptible to the fastidious recall of all the road's mishaps.

For the third time, I was traveling along the road that I had first taken with the patrol and had come back over when fleeing Don Benito. The moon had risen and numerous details brought back to mind—with a stupid, untimely and ridiculous insistence—the events of my basically lonely day. The truth was that I was exhausted, tormented by my wounds and I felt like tossing everything to the winds. But a sense of propriety kept me at Jaime's side.

I led him to the village and, in spite of my well-conceived plan, I didn't know what was going to happen and I knew even less as we got closer. My confidence had been undermined by weariness and distress. But the lack of confidence gave way to a carefree attitude and a certainty that, no matter what, the entire matter would be concluded this very night.

As I had predicted, the enemy had not followed us and had stayed in one place. Those were indeed the customs of our nation and I was probably right in thinking that all one had to do was take the opposite course of action in order to arrive at a solution. There were no unfortunate encounters as we neared the village which Jaime had told me was called Aguadulce.

We came to a halt. We had agreed that I would go into the village first, alone. But the officer, who was suspicious of me and who was none other than Fernandez, insisted on going with me and, in spite of my fondness for privacy, which seemed especially desirable these last few minutes, I told Jaime that it was better to let him come along.

From what we could hear, the "Reds" were celebrating their victory and having a ball. Fernandez did not belong to the Agreda regiment and would probably not be noticed right away. We agreed to pretend we were drunk. There were no sentries anywhere and we moved freely down the street where I had been captured. I thought again about the strange fact that Don Benito had taken the time to spot me from his bell tower and have me captured. Curious man, but I didn't want to play his games any more.

I was there to find out where he was. I was afraid that he might have left for La Paz, which was only a few miles away.

Yet my distress that longed to conclude matters kept me clutching at a stubborn hope. Fernandez was familiar with the village and assured me that the Protector was supposed to be staying at the magistrate's house. That didn't seem to be in keeping with my man's secretive nature.

The street I was familiar with was very quiet, but at the end we found ourselves in a small square which had been transformed into a camping ground and drinking bout. Around bonfires, men were eating roast lamb, were drinking copious quantities of gin, were singing, shouting and joking. There was no lack of whores and no one paid any attention to us. I trembled at the thought my guard would be recognized and so I rushed things a bit. Going up to a large, drunken sergeant, I exclaimed, "Ah, Don Benito shouldn't have left us and returned so quickly to the capital."

"By the breasts of the Virgin, you're lying! Don't tell me he left us. He's in the little monastery. I've just come back from there."

The idea of a monastery seemed plausible to me. My companion didn't know where this little monastery was, but I inquired again and, cautiously, we were able to study the entrances to the location and an out-of-the-way path by which we could bring Jaime there.

That was done without alerting the enemy during the hour that followed. Time was running out, for the night would soon be over. In spite of his pleas, a bitterly disappointed Fernandez stayed behind as head of the little band while Jaime and I, well-armed, arrived at the wall which surrounded the monastery's garden.

At that moment, sleep began to stifle the drunkards' merriment and cover the whole village. Moreover, this section had remained unaffected all this time. The wall was head-high and easy to scale. But we were afraid that sentries would be inside.

We had taken off our boots. I remember that animal-like scent which, in the chill of the night, had risen from our feet, especially from Jaime's.

In the garden, we heard a man snoring, probably the sentry, and we went toward a lighted window that I had located beforehand. The shades were lowered, but the window was open behind them. We looked very carefully inside. No one there. Without saying a word, we decided to enter the room. The doors were closed but a window opened onto another side. Onto a patio or rather a cloister. The window was closed but it seemed preferable to open that window rather than one of the doors.

It took us a while to open the window and we were unable to do this without making a little noise. After that, we discovered that a sentry was right in the middle of the inner garden and, rifle in arms, was staring dreamily at the stars while walking now and then.

Nonetheless, we moved ahead under the gallery that our window opened onto and right away we saw that the chapel was at the end of that gallery. There was some light in the chapel and the door was open to the extension of our gallery.

I started out in that direction. Jaime grabbed my arm and in the dark his gestures let me know there was nothing for us in there. Yet I insisted.

Hidden by the shadows which sheltered the entire gallery from the moon's watchful eye, we came to the door and entered a vestibule which was at the front of the chapel. A man was walking in the chapel and for a moment we didn't dare move. The even cadence of his steps, alternately coming closer and moving away, gave us the impression of someone pacing back and forth. Yet a monk would not be wearing boots and spurs. A premonition came over me or rather finally made itself clear—a long premonition that had been guiding me ever since I had stopped Jaime on the road to retreat.

We moved ahead one step at a time. I had indeed found Don Benito again—the sad and pensive Don Benito who, freely smoking his cigar, was walking from one end of the chapel to the other and back again, stopping at times in front of the altar where the candles' soft caress made a part of the gold shine.

From that moment on, I was afraid of Jaime.

I had brought him here but his every move would now seem exaggerated to me. At the very least, I believed that he could be dangerous. Because getting close to Don Benito was not going to be easy. He would have enough time to cry out and his death would most likely not save us from the same fate. What did Jaime want to do? I couldn't see his face and we didn't dare whisper.

Don Benito decided for us. Tired of walking, he sat down in a stall to one side of the altar. We were able to move closer to him by shielding ourselves within the heavier shadows along the walls. Jaime had the same idea as I did and he began to walk forward. That was a strange trip we took there in the shadows, being watched by a God who, moreover, had seen a lot worse than this. Now and then Don Benito would move in his stall and ghastly cracking noises made us freeze in our tracks. From one moment to the next, a thought stirred within me that I was not going to like Jaime's act but, nevertheless, I had wanted it and still wanted it. This act was going to seal our entire existence of recent years and make it an inalterable thought. Everything we had experienced up to now was what I had passionately desired, but not what we had in mind for later. And Don Benito? I would miss Don Benito who had cast a spell over me. If I had met Don Benito before Jaime, wouldn't I have been very fond of him? The fatal moment was drawing near. We were a few feet from our victim.

We rushed forward and Don Benito was under our pistols. Oh, woe unto us! I have seen what humanity is and how the strongest soul can be disconcerted to the core by the appearance of what is so intensely expected. No doubt that Don Benito was deeply engrossed in the most serious meditation. From what I knew about him, he had finally been laid bare by his victory. What we were bringing to him was precisely what he was contemplating in that golden cross toward which he was pointing the desolate tip of his cigar. But our theatrical gambit left him speechless.

A wave of perspiration bathed his face which, normally pale, turned an unknown color. His jaw fell slack in the sudden undoing of his pride, of his dignity. The cigar—that ultimate symbol of his consciousness—rolled across the floor tiles. His entire body, with the stupidity of a mindless animal, tried to disappear into the wood of the stall. Yes, all his nerves, in a senseless wish, were trying to become wood, they were claiming to be wood.

I looked at Jaime. He was fascinated as well. All his muscles had been tensed to steady his pistol which became the center of the situation and whose metal seemed more vibrant than our three lives.

I would like to say that I don't know what happened since the silence lasted such a long time and it seemed so impossible for it to ever end.

Suddenly, Jaime lowered his pistol and put it back in his belt. This move produced an immense revolution in Don Benito who, for a second, was flooded with hope.

Then I had an inspiration—I who thought I was destroyed, silent forever, I said, "Yes, Jaime, that's it. Give him time to get hold of himself. We surprised him. He needs time to get hold of himself. There are very few men like him."

My voice gave rise to another and just as violent movement of Don Benito's being. He regained a sort of human countenance—human, but isn't the face of death the most human?—in order to give me one of those quick, side-long glances with which he had sometimes honored me.

"Yes, yes," he murmured.

But Jaime thought he should not press his luck, no matter how certain it seemed—that luck which, during the day, he had thought struck down by the guns of Aguadulce. In place of a pistol, his hand was now holding a dagger. And suddenly he struck.

He struck harshly, accurately, squarely in the heart. While his arm was being raised, the victim's face grew immensely wider. Then, he writhed; then, he remained stunned, forever.

PART II

DOÑA CAMILLA BUSTAMENTE

I

Doña Camilla's sitting room looked out over an abyss. The Bustamentes' house, in fact, stood at the very top of the steepest district in La Paz which was hanging over a cliff. In this as in all other things, Doña Camilla had exercised her right and was occupying the room where all the day and evening lights could be captured together with the moments of silence that rose from the depths. Yet when the winds were too aggressive or lightning bolts were licking at her balcony, she would take shelter in the street-level rooms with her sisters.

One of her sisters had let Doctor Belmez marry her. As a measure of the attention he intended to bestow on me, Belmez had introduced me into this exclusive home where he was admitted, together with another son-in-law, for two of Doña Camilla's three sisters were married.

Doña Camilla, who had taken back the name of Bustamente, had been married herself—which seemed even more incredible now than at the time when it had occurred. What man had been able to conquer such a beautiful fiancée—so proud, so intolerant?

Her entire family—in which there were only women—lived for her alone. Kingdom of the Amazons. Nonetheless, it was here that one could see the most ample bosoms in all La Paz. There was even a majestic reminder of this in the mother's sagging chest. At the theater it was a popular pasttime to be on the lookout for those multiple treasures, haughtily retreating beneath their mantillas, at the back of the most beautiful box.

Kingdom of the Amazons because of pride and disdain. Convent as well because of the lust for spiritual matters which prevailed in this isolated region where, moreover, only the heart's superstitions were obeyed as a last resort. Gynaeceum finally, inasmuch as the husbands of two of the Bustamentes were present and had been granted permission to impregnate their wives as often as possible. But men, children, animals and servants existed only for Doña Camilla.

Having given up all hope of finding a hero—sharing in this the common lot of virgins—she had married the first man to ask her. She had accepted him because for a few days she had thought he was handsome and intelligent. Yet beauty does not last in the eyes of the person who, needing something more, realizes that the lamp has no oil. Well in advance of the fatal ceremony, Camilla had known that she was making a mistake. Yet she had not backed out, telling herself it would be better to go through with it once and for all. She considered herself to be untouchable. The thick-headed stallion had wanted to exercise his right. She had pretended to give in, then had energetically thrown him out. In short, after a few days of brooding, there were unforgivable scenes. Camilla hit him in the head with a piece of silverware and, as a result, the intruder was killed outright.

The story of an accident, disseminated by the family, had fooled no one in La Paz, but had been accepted by everyone.

Afterward, Camilla had closed herself off with her sisters in the isolation which had previously been her delight. An isolation partially receptive to outside curiosities and admirations, a wild and mushy isolation—childish and serious, weighted down with music, books, candy, laughter and little girls' arguments. They never went out except to go to church and sometimes to the theater or to leave town every year and travel to their favorite *estancia* on the way to Santa Cruz. They had gone to Europe for two years and it was there Camilla was said to have taken a lover.

She would arrange to meet those men who might be expected to show some interest, but, as a rule, she didn't see them again after their first visit. Each in turn was rumored to be her lover, but the few people who were close to her swore that, out of spite, she was as virtuous as her sisters—two of whom were mothers and the youngest. … But I shall discuss the youngest sister later on.

Camilla's greatest passion was music and it was because of my guitar that I was invited to her home as well as elsewhere. I succeeded in being asked back. I was delighted to discover this small oasis in the middle of a desert. There were only a few dubious places, bursting with working-class merriment, where I could feel so much at ease. The people of one's country can be appreciated only at both extremes —among a few simple folk and among a few esthetes who at times rediscover simplicity through self-denial and then transmit it to you with unusual insight—all the more unusual for us since they have retained, deep within their hearts, the original source of passion.

The four Bustamente sisters were beautiful. For a few weeks I was dazed, surrounded by this whirlwind of physical charms and graces, of squandered nobility, of purity as indecent as a child's womb, of intuitions as implacable as the horseshoe that leaves its print in the dust, of laughter to arouse both evil spirits and angels.

They knew everything and they knew nothing. They were daring in every way and swore like mule drivers and blushed over silly nothings their fancy invented. On the whole, they were all admirably pale with dark red lips.

But Camilla's complexion, to be sure, was paler than the others' by virtue of its moon-fruit, velvety texture and its evening-rose opulence. She was very tall and very powerful and in danger of being slightly overweight because she remained inactive ten months of the year—although at the *estancia* she rode with all the unbridled delight of an Amazon. Her eyes would have been perhaps excessively lustrous if they had not been veiled by a near-sighted softness. Her forehead was as hard as the pediment of a palace. Her teeth were a sign of vigorous health, a secular challenge.

In a portrait it would be most useful to suggest anatomical measurements, to be able to reveal the inner harmony of a body's bone structure. Only therein does deep beauty lie—a proud equilibrium seated at the center of a serenely proportioned skull, thorax and pelvis. Camilla was a noble architecture, austere in her voluptuousness like a palace by Vignole—something I didn't understand, and then very bitterly, until much later when I went to Italy. However, right away I had known that her ultimate virtue was attuned to the solemn tones of my guitar.

Whenever I saw her hands and feet, I would bless the cruelty of her family who for three centuries had exploited the Indians in order to insure the idle perfection of these so very delicate and strong fingers. What's more, the Indians had been downtrodden before— nevertheless, in accordance with their Indian law—and they will continue to be so according to any law whatever.

Camilla's fingers were admirable at the piano. She introduced me to European music of which I knew almost nothing. Once again, I nearly lost control of my senses and it took me quite a while to get back to normal. I was then able myself to invest her with my knowledge of the Indian folk song. I had wandered at length over our high plateaus, collecting the heart-rending debris of an art which was the very secret of this impossible land, lost in the midst of excess—but there is no excess which is still not moderation for the race of men who roam between the fartherest limits of their domain.

Camilla was deeply moved and finally came to know that race of people among whom her own race of people were living. I also came to know them better, even though Camilla—through everything she was teaching me about her people—almost made me lose contact with them. Those were tumultuous hours, assailed by impetuous winds like the ones which came to strike the very delicately latched windows, hanging over the sheer drop of the Indian precipice.

It would be pointless to deny that I was consumed with desire. Yet the other forces that had been endlessly devouring me could fight like a back fire against this blaze. I was ugly—wretchedly so—and condemned to the lowest of prostitutes. I was both a theologian and musician as well. I knew how to control my eyes and I had practiced this moreover on Conception with a marvelous cruelty. I despised women as much as Father Florida and when I said to myself, the first time I had seen Camilla: "And yet, the person who lives in this magnificent palace, among the radiant strength of lines, is only a small, futile bird, caged up in some nook," these were not idle words. In an instant all of Camilla's charm was wiped out, just as for her the charm of my guitar was devastated whenever she looked up and saw my despicable lips.

My desire could also be dispersed and weakened among the other Bustamente sisters. They were all beautiful and their proximity gave lavish proof to the frightening idea that beauty was always different and always the same. I grew progressively sluggish from the exhausting alternation of poisons and antidotes.

Augusta, who had married Belmez, seemed made of innocence—an indestructible innocence which surpassed the vision of her mating with the doctor. Having seen her, one could no longer see in him anything but the ephemeral representative of the male sex, stripped of the power to leave its mark.

There were times when I had to put up with him—something which hardly appealed to me because over a period of time ridiculous characters are entertaining only on the stage. Belmez was one of those large men who are insipid by dent of intestinal satisfaction. The bovine health they enjoy makes them believe they have the strength of a bull, and furthermore gives them intellectual pretentions. Belmez had regularly stood all the examinations for medicine and Freemasonry; as a result, he looked upon women and men as easy objects to consume. All the more so since he had heard that deviousness also existed. Thus, by winking an eye, he really thought that he not only understood but was also misleading everyone.

Had he himself—an average, middle-class citizen and physician whose office was in fact no more than a shop—not succeeded in becoming a part of the Bustamente family? Did he not reign as an attentive and prolific husband in the bedroom of one of the four most beautiful people in La Paz? Moreover, was he not unfaithful to her with every female client who was worth the risk and with the wives of several high-ranking lodge brothers?

How had he gained access to so many attractive comforts? Those are the idiotic secrets of Freemasonry whose worth I did not appreciate until much later.

Belmez had set his sights on Jaime and me. What had he gotten from Jaime in the beginning? I didn't know and my lack of knowledge —justified perhaps by the absence of information—was the only thing which permitted me to have a little respect for the doctor; otherwise, I disapproved of him as the only trace of vulgarity in a group where, without him, there would have been only light-hearted charm and brilliant simplicity. I blamed him more for darkening now and then the peaceful aura of Augusta than for sometimes deflowering, for an entire evening, by a single word, an idea with a woman's body. Nothing was more annoying than to meet a fool in this garden of flesh and spirit where I would have liked to be alone. Belmez would barge into Camilla's sitting room from time to time where, nonetheless, he had been forbidden to come, so he could speak to me about Pimander while encircling Augusta's waist with a victorious stump.

By the mild glimmer—the almost colorless display of her sensuousness—the other sister also stood apart from the imprecise figure of the husband who was bound to her. She received pleasurable attentions from a handsome man just as the earth receives rain with an enormous benevolence which nothing could limit. Augusta and Rosalba were surrounded by a swarm of children like small guardian angels.

As for the youngest sister who was not married, it was a different story. She was living without protection, without the safeguard of children and husband, under the absolute influence of Camilla. That influence—exerted upon a person who perhaps deserved to live by herself—seemed to me unjust. It was the sight of this completely destroyed Isabel that gave me the strength to resist the prestige of Camilla's beauty—which, after all, was only that of a woman.

I saw Isabel suffer, living with Camilla, from a revered and incurable illness. Although just as beautiful in her basic structure, she seemed less so because she had long ago given up adding beauty on top of beauty. She had felt this to be a pointless desecration of life even though her sister was already that way and she could hardly admit to herself that she was only a very submissive, very meekly distant echo of Camilla.

I moved closer to Isabel in the hope—which I thought was concealed—of catching sight of such a complete surrender. I was wondering if my concern wouldn't extract some cry of revolt from her against her sister or at the very least an admission of the situation. But she was forewarned about such plans and she tendered an official rejection prepared with malicious and impeccable skill. She was hiding her breasts in a nun-like hallucination.

My intentions were so precisely discouraged that they faded away and, encouraged by Isabel herself, I once again fell under Camilla's immediate spell.

All this had made me very forgetful of Jaime. The fact was that, since Don Benito's death, we had moved apart from one another. When he had come to power, without much trouble, he had sent for me and told me about his dilemma.

"You don't want to be a minister and you won't take money. Do you just want a clergyman's stipend?"

Like me, he thought that at least one of his followers should not be corrupted by any reward—and that person could only be me. There was a profound need in this because my own hands were covered with Don Benito's blood even more than his. A few months later, however, two or three magnificent guitars arrived from Spain. A special envoy had bought them from the family of an Andalusian artist, recently deceased, who had previously traveled through South America and whom I had praised to Jaime.

I wasn't the least bit interested in what Jaime was doing in office; however, I could never forget his presence more than a few weeks. And so, not a month went by that I didn't come to his palace around midnight. Those were the evenings when, by a secret agreement, he would be free. Then, for two hours he would listen to me and my guitar.

As a prelude, I would play a few notes and begin to discuss matters that seemed far removed from politics. He loathed books because he considered them dead like those who valued them. Moreover, it was too late for him to read that necessary quantity of works which eventually liberate educated minds who then no longer come into contact with the written word except when, as pensive strollers, they move a stone in their path with the tip of their cane. I related the history of the world to him—composed effortlessly on his behalf. My mind entered his own for all eternity and only had to appear with grace and simplicity in order to find its fertilization site. I would tell him something and suspect—although he didn't give any sign of pleasure nor even show much confidence in me—that he would some day do other things with it. During this premonition my guitar would often produce tones which clashed with my words.

The idea came to mind that I had to bring together the two people who held my attention in life. That would not be easy since Camilla belonged to one of the leading families and the nobles were committed, for the most part, to the party of the "Reds" that Jaime had conquered in the person of Don Benito. As they watched Jaime curry the favor of the common people, they conducted themselves with the most hostile restraint toward him.

Yet was Camilla not in the habit of doing what she pleased and was she not assured of her family's indulgence?

II

Would Jaime want to see Camilla? He had made Conchita come back to La Paz and had set her up in a rather beautiful house, very near the palace. She seemed entirely conquered—as much by the savage beating and imprisonment he had made her endure as by his victory which she had never thought possible. She had nonetheless been victorious in her own way. Since he had not killed her, she concluded that he never would. But this feeling stayed hidden in her heart for a long time. She admired Jaime for the moment and was proud of him.

She was more impressed by the aura of fame than by money. Her new house was just as filthy as her previous hovels. Her cigarette butts were still burning holes in the rugs as well as her dresses which were lying all over—crumpled as soon as she put them on. She ate, drank, put on weight and complained that Jaime didn't come around often enough to make love to her.

He seemed more in love than ever before and he was the one who would truly suffer, at certain times, from his all too brief visits. He had taken over, however, with a surprising sense of duty. He would not have deprived his ministers of a single minute of audience time and he saw an unbelievable number of favor-seekers who hurried forth from every province because the rumor of his simple ways and decency had quickly spread. It must be said that he was just as quick with a kick in the rear as he was with a handout and that he was shrewdly vigilant in spite of all his liberal generosity. The cowardice and baseness that Don Benito's followers had displayed—just like his own supporters' rapacity—had taught him a great deal about the way men become obsequious whenever circumstances dictate.

It was through gossip alone that these characteristics had gotten back to me, for I paid no attention at all to his activities on a day-by-day basis. One night, I brought myself to talk to him about Camilla.

"Now, why do you want me to see that silly girl?"

"Because she's beautiful."

"Conchita's enough for me."

"Look, I'm not trying to offer you a woman. I would like you to talk to her. Through her you would get to know how the nobles think and learn how to protect yourself better against them."

"I know who they are. They hate me, but that doesn't matter because they are cowards. How many of them fought in Don Benito's army? They're too squeamish to take up arms."

"They're even more dangerous since, from now on, these cowards will be your most dangerous enemies. But you have to get to know them beyond their cowardice, and besides, Camilla isn't a coward."

I explained to him how I had met her and what delightful pleasures had been mine in that house.

"If you make an ally of her, the nobles will be upset."

I plunged a little foolishly into this political allegation.

He looked at me sarcastically.

"You're quite a politician."

"No. I'm fond of you and Camilla. I want to bring together the two people I love."

"I'll think about it," he said as he showed me out.

But he didn't pursue my suggestion. I hadn't said anything to Camilla, knowing that I could very well hurt her if I failed and that she was more thin-skinned than a cat.

One day, I came across Father Florida at Camilla's.

Having lost interest in political intrigue, I hadn't seen him for quite some time; yet I knew he was watching Jaime's movements and, although preserving an enigmatic attitude, he was taking part in the secret discussions of the nobles. He had been Camilla's spiritual advisor when she was a girl, but since then she had stopped seeing him. Even though she went to church and took Easter communion, she professed a romantic Christian faith which was very unorthodox. She would see him at times, nevertheless, because she was amused by the man's icy-tempered and witty meanness.

I guessed right away that he had come to observe my relationship with the beautiful young woman. I was so disgusted by his obnoxious curiosity that I had no trouble hiding this desire from him—the one who knew so well, moreover, how to control himself.

Suddenly, he asked, "Our friend Felipe must be telling you a lot about Don Jaime?"

He was one of the first whom I heard give the Protector the respectful title of *Don* which is given only to members of the oldest families.

"Yes," Camilla answered, "he talks to me about him and it puzzles me, because I feel that Felipe is too observant to be mistaken even about those he likes. He sings his praises to me which is hard to believe according to the impressions I've formed about the man."

"He will have you meet him and you can judge for yourself."

At the same time Father Florida gave me that quick and piercing look which was his major strength. He had therefore guessed what my intentions were and was scheming around them. I wondered if a careless remark by Doctor Behnez, in whose presence one evening I had the misfortune of letting a word slip, might not have gotten back to him in a roundabout manner—because, in his own way, the doctor seemed to be counting on bringing together his in-laws and Jaime, who, no doubt, was staying too far beyond the Mason's influence.

"At any rate," Camilla went on, "if I should see Jaime Torrijos, it would be very hard to make conversation because I detest politics and he must be one of those men who can speak of nothing else."

"He likes music and dancing," Father Florida murmured, referring to Conchita.

"He likes dancers and that's not the same thing as dancing," she scoffed with a disinterested expression that seemed forced to me.

"Well now," I exclaimed, "he also likes musicians. And let me tell you that if he likes them, it's because he likes music."

"Yes, there is that, it's true," Camilla said, looking at me. She liked more than just music in me, of course, but her friendship was terribly strained by my ugliness. At that point, however, she was beginning to overcome that uneasiness and since she was no doubt seeing me with another man for the first time, the moral fear she felt in Father Florida's presence helped her to be more openly affectionate toward me.

"Yes," she continued, "bring him to me, Felipe."

I shook my head vaguely.

"What? He doesn't want to see me?"

"He's shy, well—unsociable."

"Bah!"

Father Florida had succeeded in provoking her—something I had not dreamed of doing.

Some time later, Conchita, who was bored because Jaime had forbidden her to dance and who ate too much, fell seriously ill. That renewed my courage enough so I could try out my plan.

Just as she seemed to be getting better, Conchita left for the country. Jaime sent for me more often during the few moments he had free and which he had recently spent with a fever-stricken mistress. I spoke to him again about Camilla and suddenly he agreed to see her.

I was excited about this meeting and I injected a little of my excitement into the nonetheless impavid nerves of my friend. All this brought on a nasty mood which, at the last minute, almost ruined everything. As though trying to leave before getting there, he swung his horse around on the very street where Camilla lived—a street that climbed rather steeply by lengthy degrees. But, at last he got there.

Camilla's dresses were extraordinarily simple in design. The one she was wearing that day was no more than a large, soft swirl of black silk which clung in a suggestive, even languorous fashion to the swell of her breasts and sloping back. She was wearing no jewelry other than a few diamonds that clasped her chignon low on her neck.

I suddenly felt afraid when I saw these two individuals facing each other. They constituted my entire universe. Instead of telling myself that my universe was made of silence and that not a single word need be spoken just then, I was seized with panic and, in a choked voice, I suggested playing some music.

"Please do," Camilla murmured.

She sang an Indian song I had taught her and Jaime was surprised. He looked at her suspiciously and the admiration that was gradually beginning to show remained subdued.

"Nevertheless, you don't know the Indians," he blurted out when she had finished.

"No, but I should."

"You don't know our people."

"They don't know me."

Jaime frowned.

"And do *you* know them?" she murmured.

"I am one of them."

"Aren't you playing with words?"

"You can see that I am one of the common people."

"You aren't like my cousins, but that doesn't prove that you are still one of the common people."

"If I were no longer one of the common people, then I would no longer be anything at all."

"You would be yourself."

He shook his head. He wanted to say something.

"Jaime isn't like you," I said, "someone who escapes. He's attached."

"Yes, that's right," Jaime grumbled in a half-satisfied tone of voice.

Camilla gave me an attentive look that she slowly turned toward Jaime.

"I'm attached to everything through music."

"So there," I exclaimed too impetuously, "you are also attached to Jaime."

"Perhaps."

Silence fell and we accepted it. I played softly for a while to bless this silence that turned out to be a fortunate occurrence, full of promises.

After the meeting, I was very anxious to learn the impressions of the two participants. I left with Jaime who admitted she was beautiful but who would not agree to say anything else. As for Camilla, whom I went to see the next day, all she wanted to talk about as well was the Protector's handsome demeanor.

"He has some Indian blood for sure," she said, as if to defend herself.

"They say that about everybody. I don't think that's true. But, moreover, there's more to it than just blood—there's the air of our country. To be sure, on these high plateaus we have been breathing, for three hundred years, the same air as the Indians who also came here from other places."

Jaime came back several times and it became a habit. Jaime and Camilla acted as though they had been warned of my intentions and they tried hard to avoid in their speech and gestures anything that might appear to be a sign of surrender or seduction. Nonetheless, the fact was that they were spending hours together and that could not be done with impunity. In view of each one's unyielding character, if they had not been repulsed at first, they could only fall gradually into each other's arms. That seemed inevitable to me and I was waiting for that inevitability to come about.

Camilla was alive in Jaime's presence and day after day she displayed one movement of her body after another. She would play the piano, sing, pour coffee for her visitor. She would move about the sitting room and with each stride the terrific motion of her thighs spread an irresistible influence all around. She would lean over her balcony and her breasts would then be suspended over the chasm while the back of her neck would bend under her bluish hair pinned down with diamonds.

I grew less and less noticeable and my heart was torn apart by a desperate anticipation and admiration. Should I no longer be present? Yes, it was time for me to disappear. But they both seemed to fear my leaving. Each time, they asked me to come again the next time and I was afraid that I might regrettably disturb the progress of their love.

There was, however, a time when I was suspicious of myself. Wasn't I lingering in their presence because I couldn't tear myself away from the sight of Camilla? And who knows—wasn't it even to put off Jaime's victory?

I had nonetheless wanted this victory just like his victory over Don Benito. In the end, I failed to come one day to the regular meeting.

A few days later, the most difficult thing I had to do was return to Camilla's house. I was afraid of being irreverently curious by looking at her face and body since I knew that this would mean extracting a confession from her. Not that I thought anything improper would have taken place between my two heroes, but I was very certain that what they had already said to each other in front of me in a soft murmur of suggestive words would have been stated during a moment of silence and irreparably so.

She certainly did not try to mislead me. She asked me to play some music with her and she became so distracted that she stopped playing and let her hands rest motionless on the keys for a long time. I was grateful to her for this show of confidence that calmed my scruples.

I adhered to the obligation of visiting her from time to time, but I put off seeing Jaime. This was the only way I could prove my determination to be discreet. If I had seen both of them, I would have occupied all the approaches to the isolation that was forming around them and from which I had to remove myself as far as possible.

III

It was a short while later. I had taken leave of La Paz to go on one of those wandering journeys to the most remote of Indians tribes without which life would have been impossible for me. I had given in to that marvelous and fertile fascination for whatever I was unfamiliar with and didn't understand but around which I would construct visions of my most intimate wishes.

If their songs haunted me, became a part of me, it had nothing to do with blood ties, because there is not one drop of Indian blood in me. But is it possible to live, after a succession of ancestors, in a land without being influenced by the spirit of this land? They say that the Indians themselves have not lived forever on our high plateaus, that they came from somewhere else, from Asia. Yet, in the end, they became a part of this land and I myself am a part of this land. There are as many secret bonds between all the spirits of a land as there are antagonistic forces. When I speak of the earth's spirits, I am not contrasting them with the spirits of the sky. Because the sky is just as much with us as the earth—especially in our country where we live in one as well as the other.

In addition to their songs, I was crazy about their coats. Oh, those Indian coats! I could feel their many colors vibrate on my senses like the strings of my guitar. I needed to intoxicate myself in the cluster of their cries, in the polyphony of their wailing. I stuffed myself, intoxicated myself with the heartrending and reassuring contrast that these garish coats made with the grey tones of the high plateaus that winter had laid bare. A history professor—the fool!—told me one day that these colors could not have been created by the Indians except in other climes, in tropical valleys, and they had existed as a matter of course in our elevated wilderness. What he had assumed in this instance was contrary to life. The Indians produced these stripes and jagged markings by overtaxing the weakened, distressed shades of the high plateaus from a need to ward off the threat of nothingness. If they hadn't extracted these colors from their bowels, they would have fallen prey to the inhuman ordeal of extreme altitude. Inhuman, yet still human since man was able to tailor his reaction to it. The coca that the Indians consume is also, by its intimate excesses, just the right compensation for the savage burden of these heights, and in the end it is only bread and life.

I had therefore, once again, lived in the most cunning and truest manner in the midst of Indian stench and lice, of Indian degradation and eternity. It should be said as well that only with an Indian woman was my ugliness no longer important; yet that did not debase my soul which remained just as closely linked with the race of conquerors, the Spanish. All those things cannot be expressed and my guitar itself has been able to express them only two or three times.

When I returned to La Paz, I informed Jaime that I was in town. I suddenly had this powerful urge to see him again. Right away I received at home an urgent invitation, signed by the Protector's personal secretary, to attend a party he was giving that very evening at the governmental palace. I was stunned. First of all, what a way to treat me! And what's more, a party! Jaime had never thought of anything like this before and he had been roundly criticized for having turned the palace into a deserted place where, in one corner, he had pitched camp.

Since there was no time to inquire about anything, I responded to the invitation like a transient stranger. It was already late. In the wide-open reception rooms, I detected a certain mood that astonished me. There were very few people present and those attending all belonged to the nobility as well as the most important families who, until now, had certainly never set foot in the palace. The men were there with their wives and they all seemed tense and anxious. I had known them all for quite some time. Our customs are very simple and very unpretentious, and under different circumstances, I would not have been at all uncomfortable, finding myself in the company of these people. But I had already noticed, before going away, that in aristocratic circles I was being avoided somewhat insomuch as I was thought to be closely associated with the Protector. Tonight, as a result, I could not let myself do anything that might denote the slightest eagerness. With an indifferent look, I moved through the large reception rooms where everyone was standing almost still and silent. I wanted to see Jaime but he wasn't there. What did all this mean? I didn't know whom to ask because I could see no one except those I didn't care to approach.

Indeed, it was strange—that gathering of men and women who seemed haughty, insulted and almost frightened. I had scarcely been there for fifteen minutes and already I was feeling a sense of uneasiness, almost anguish. What was in store for us? What had happened in La Paz while I was gone? I felt guilty for having stayed away so long and not having tried to keep informed.

Suddenly, things began to stir in the room which adjoined Jaime's office—Don Benito's former office; Jaime was entering.

Jaime was no longer the same. Something had happened How could my nerves not have sensed this from afar? Jaime had aged. I had never seen his face so distorted, so lined, nor especially his eyes flash with such a feverish and malevolent awareness. There was something of Don Benito's look in his expression.

Followed by two or three officers, he strode vigorously to the center of the first reception room and one of his ministers, who for tonight was acting as master of ceremonies, presented all the nobles who were there to him, one after the other. Because of Jaime's stationary position, they were forced to come toward him with their wives. He was dressed in military attire, in his Agreda uniform, and in front of him he was holding a heavy cavalry saber. He calmly scrutinized each person that greeted him and he bowed slightly to the women. In their presence, a strange smile came to his lips on which there was the usual respect and a threatening irony. As that sort of ceremony was coming to an end, I saw one of Camilla's cousins step forward. I suddenly thought about her and just at that moment I saw her walking toward Jaime on the arm of the other cousin whose name was Manuelito. She must have arrived well after me, for I had seen neither her nor any member of her family until now.

Her appearance did not seem to have been planned on the program of "festivities" since Jaime was startled when he saw her come toward him. I understood that something had happened between them, and most likely unpleasant or even painful, because they faced each other with closed and hardened expressions. On the other hand, everyone was watching them in an avid and also breathless manner.

Just after they had exchanged a barely discernible greeting, the doors to a large hall were opened, doors which until then had remained closed. Inside, we saw a large number of chairs arranged so they were facing a raised platform. All the people there seemed surprised by that theatrical setting. To me it was obvious that not a single person knew exactly why he was invited and each one suspected that nothing good would come of this mysterious development.

Jaime motioned with his hand and the nobles moved toward their seats. The first ones to enter seemed willing to sit only in the rear, far from the platform, but the last to arrive had to move down to the very front rows. Jaime had virtually herded everybody ahead of him and he went to station himself to one side of the audience while standing erect and continuing to level at everyone that chilly smile which was slowly becoming a rigid smirk. The officers who accompanied him had stayed near the door which was now closed.

The stage had been positioned in front of a door which was hidden by a curtain. That curtain was raised and a guitarist entered who placed a stool on the stage and sat down. It was then that I had an inkling of what was going to happen and the reason why Camilla's presence was so unusual.

I looked around for her. She was sitting, clearly in view, in the middle of the audience and not far from Jaime who could capture all her facial expressions. Camilla's features were impassive, but her eyes were open wide.

The guitarist began to play. The audience was whispering and I could see, that many people like me had guessed. They seemed extremely upset and displeased, and some of them were glancing longingly at the door.

The curtain went up—and Conchita-Conception entered. Conception in a magnificent dancer's costume, wearing a mask. She was wearing a mask. She also had a large shawl over her shoulders which hid them completely as though the result of a sudden modesty —an extravagant defiance.

The mask disconcerted the gathering. That was a clever idea which, for the moment at least, created an uneasy mood for the "festivities."

The hall was lighted by an enormous number of candles and beneath the shawl the bottom part of Conception's dress, recently shipped from Spain no doubt, sparkled and glistened. She gave a deep bow and beneath the mask I saw her tightly drawn lips.

She began to dance. Her first steps were going to shatter, so it seemed, in the frightened and hostile silence like a glass in which water had frozen. But just imagining this was to grow panicky and forget Conception's pride, Jaime's pride. Was it necessary, furthermore, to call by the name of pride the strong feeling of their sheer animality which lifted these two beings up—her a dancer and him a cavalryman—in the midst of all these seated people?

She danced. No, she wasn't dancing. That wasn't a dance. Of all future sun dances, it was scarcely the murky embryo, unforeseeable in an underground world. Wrapped in her immense and dark-colored shawl, whose folds she had first gently shaken down to the very bottom of her glistening dress, while covering her head with it at the same time, she was stamping imperceptibly in one place, without the slightest noise from her heels. Under the suddenly dimmed lights, she was black, enigmatic, both offended, overwhelmed and threatening.

This was not something Spanish, but Indian. I recognized the most elementary, the slowest and most silent motif of funeral magic. It was a dark and relentless concentration that plunged the spirit into an ineffable, uncertain area between death and birth, anger and resignation, pain and repose. That lasted a long time, a very long time, too long a time. It would never come to an end.

The guitarist, an Indian I didn't recognize, was first-rate, with a seemingly rudimentary and rough style. He was so accomplished in his playing that I put aside all envy and lost myself in his art. As for the audience, already disconcerted by the mask, it was disarmed by the strange solemnity of this performance. At best, it could macerate the glum uncertainty of its emotion.

Bit by bit the reticent shudder, forever interrupted just as it was about to free that shapeless mass from a tremendous inability to express anything at all, gnawed away at the silence like waves lapping at a boulder. The interminable muted sound of the guitar grew sharper. Now and then groping movements raised the opaque mass of the shawl. A far distant drumming of heels heralded some event. But suddenly, on a harsh note from the guitar, everything stopped. And she was motionless again. Absolute stillness for a moment—yes, absolute in spite of the guitar's playing again, as though the black mass were indeed nothing more than discouragement or rejection, or labor forever ended. Then, by a succession of tiny jerks, we understood that this immobility was misleading just like the previous trembling and that it was produced by an inner vibration which became a part of all of us without our realizing it.

The audience was totally captivated, oblivious to everything, wrapped in the spell of the shawl. Thus, there were two or three undulations within the long horizontal line of the motif, and then everything stopped again, and for good. The surprised audience remained stunned. In a second, Conception—because it was her, I told myself like a man hesitating between illusion and reality—had disappeared behind the curtain.

No one applauded. There was a feeling that it was impossible to applaud. Eyes turned toward Jaime to find out ... But just then the guitar struck up a more lively tune and Conception came back, still wearing a mask, still wrapped up, but this time in a red shawl, and she began a more human dance. She danced longer, more powerfully than any woman had ever danced. People forgot everything: who they were, why they had come, Jaime's presence, where they were, who Conception was. They applauded violently, with a somber violence as though they were plunging with voluptuous abandon into the unpredictable and irritating quality of the situation.

Occasionally I would look at Jaime. For some time now, he had lost that initial icy smile and I saw again a little of that tortured and hunted expression he had before when he attended Conception's performance for the Agreda officers or the dragoons. But that was now mixed with an expression of tough and calm defiance.

Suddenly, the last dance was over. Conception bowed as she did in the beginning and, standing back up, she suddenly took off her mask and at the same time dropped the last of the shawls she had laid one over the other on her shoulders and which her hands had never removed. She stood almost naked down to her waist. Her two magnificent breasts, covered with perspiration, were glistening with their nipples erect from moral excitement.

There was an enormous outcry of surprise but also of admiration. It was impossible for this small crowd to regain its composure and it could only applaud wildly, admitting it had fallen completely into the trap. Jaime had moved rapidly forward through the chairs and was now at the stage. He extended his hand to Conception on whose face there was more exhaustion than satisfaction. But Jaime's gesture revived her instantly and, jumping from the stage, she moved with him into the midst of the nobles. Among these, especially the women, there was an immediate, slight recoil, but it was too late. So, one after the other, all our noble lords had to bow to the dancer and their wives had to nod their heads. Conception, however, was not satisfied with that alone and she held out a hand that the men had to kiss, that the women had to shake.

As I witnessed that, my mood changed. It seemed to me , that the original idea of the ceremony had been striking, highly effective, but that now everything was being ruined. The way Jaime and Conception looked heightened my impression. They were displaying an overly, smug satisfaction in spreading humiliation around them. And when, as they moved forward and indulged their whims like undisciplined children, they sensed hostility rising up around them again, they showed an even greater defiance and scorn.

But Camilla? I had forgotten about her throughout the evening. I imagined that everything had been arranged so that this would happen. I saw her among the chairs, surrounded by her cousins who could scarcely contain their indignation that she was there and that they were there. She was very pale but held her head up high, lowering her eyelids at times over her eyes which grew wider and wider and seemed to be hurting her.

Jaime and Conception, moving from one person to the next, were circling the small group of the Bustamentes. Were they finally going to approach them? I was very much afraid so and everyone was awaiting this moment with anxious curiosity.

Neither Jaime nor Conception was looking at Camilla. But suddenly they were face to face. Jaime had taken Conception by the hand again and, pointing to her in an almost brutal manner, he said to Camilla, "You can see. Doña Camilla, that a daughter of the people has everything she could want. She feels and knows everything."

He was obviously referring to something that Camilla had said to him. What had happened between them? While at first seeming to be dominated by curiosity and the pleasure of defeating a woman she certainly considered to be her rival, Conception now seemed unhappy with Jaime's manner and tried to pull her hand away from his. But he was holding it very tightly. Conception was angry at the way he was looking at Camilla even as he was saying what he was saying to her.

The cousins were abashed, expecting some open insult, and did not know what to think. Yet they gathered around Camilla with a look of vague defiance.

Camilla had closed her eyes for a long while. Finally, she said, "I like the people where they are at present. They are not suited for living in palaces."

One sensed that this was not what she would have preferred to say. But she had found nothing else and, by the assurance in her voice, she indicated she was satisfied with it.

"The people can live anywhere," Jaime loudly exclaimed, suddenly addressing all the nobles. "They can live in their government's palace. All their strength and beauty are within themselves. Look!"

His voice had grown huskier with each word and everything he had been holding back from the very start of the evening erupted.

And it was for the purpose of this anticipated explosion that he had arranged this entire show. With his last word, he had taken on a wild look and his violent gesture, suddenly and provocatively vulgar, showed his mistress' breasts to everyone.

Disapproving whispers were heard and one of Camilla's cousins cried out, while making a move as if to spare her a disgraceful sight: "Are we going to let decent women be insulted?"

Jaime lunged toward him. "Decent woman! What does that mean? Do you want me to tell you what a decent woman is?"

"Jaime!" Conception's voice hoarsely called out.

Jaime moved back and looked at her. The disorderly seizure within him was instantly quieted. He said almost calmly to Conception, "Now, they've seen you. I'm going to take you home."

Conception was divided among the most diverse emotions, all of which she managed to repress.

He took another long, sweeping look about him, now almost indifferent, then slowly walked away with her through the reception rooms. His spurs glittered behind him.

Stifled and gasping for breath, the crowd soon drifted out. Camilla was now showing her grief, sadness, and regret. She seemed hostile to everything people were saying to her from all sides, totally vague and babbling moreover, in the guise of condolences.

IV

What had happened between Jaime and Camilla? That is what I would have liked to find out right then and there as I was leaving the palace. That small crowd could have undoubtedly furnished me with explanations but they would have been false in some way or another. I had left without getting near Jaime who, however, must have seen me but, carried away by his passions, wasn't at all interested in my opinion.

That left only Camilla from whom I could learn at least half the truth. Although afraid that I had suddenly become a stranger to her I went to her house the next day. She refused to see me, but her sisters greeted me warmly.

I took Isabel to one side. Before I could ask her any questions, she questioned me about what had taken place in the palace. The cousins were saying that Camilla had been insulted by the Protector and they were displaying the greatest anger and an unmistakable wish for revenge but she hadn't understood precisely what the insult consisted of. Through me, she was at last going to know what to believe.

"Well, what did he say to her, Felipe? Is it true he told her that Conchita was a more respectable woman than she was?"

Isabel was disgusted by the incident, but also by her curiosity about the incident, because that curiosity could only be an indiscretion in regard to her sister.

"No, he didn't say that."

I gave her an accurate account—that is, disappointing in its seriousness. She nodded her head. I tried to finish, "I got the impression that this entire spectacle was organized because of what Camilla might have said earlier against Conception, during an argument with Jaime, which probably ended in their separation. But at the same time, there was no deliberate premeditation against her since he seemed completely surprised to see her at the palace."

"But, in fact, she was the one who wanted to go. She wasn't invited. She forced her cousins to take her. There was a scene here."

"But did she know what was going to happen?"

Isabel hesitated for a moment. I tried hard to seem unconcerned, which made her smile. She continued, "She had received a note that had deeply troubled her. It was then that she decided to go to the palace."

I said nothing.

"I don't know who sent the note."

"Do you think she knew that Conception would be shown off the way she was?"

She made an uncertain gesture but I saw that she believed it. Camilla had thus acted out of jealous curiosity. Asking any more questions would be difficult.

With her lips tightened somewhat, Isabel had started to dream. It was obvious that she was letting herself freely observe in my presence what had taken place between Jaime and Camilla, that she knew about everything; it was also clear that she didn't want to tell me, but that perhaps in the long run she would let me guess. How had she learned about it? I couldn't believe that Camilla would have confided in her. Had she spied on Camilla? Had there been violent scenes in the house? At any rate, I was very determined, by not putting any question to her, to punish her for the way she had let my curiosity dangle in mid-air.

"In all likelihood," I went on in a light-hearted manner, "we will never know anything about all that. What's more, I'll never mention a word of this to Jaime."

"What, you haven't discussed it with him?" she exclaimed with a disappointed expression.

I saw that she was expecting me to give her some information about Jaime that the Bustamentes probably didn't have. I was going to answer naively that I hadn't even tried to see him alone but I realized that, in order to obtain my secrets, she would give me her own. Therefore, I nodded my head in an enigmatic way. I added with sincere distress, "What will come of all this? Now Jaime is in serious trouble with the nobles. He hates them as much as they hate him. There's going to be bloodshed."

"My cousins are crazy. When they got back from the palace, they wanted to leave La Paz and–"

She seemed to regret having said so much. To reassure her, I continued, "But what does Camilla think of all this? I'll admit that what she answered Jaime surprised me a lot. For her–who has such scorn for politics–to have suddenly talked about the "people" in that manner. It's true she said almost anything since she wasn't able to say what was really on her mind."

Isabel smiled with a rather bitter irony. "Yes, you're right. She didn't say what she would have liked to say. She wasn't able to."

"She wasn't able to?"

Once again, we were on the verge of the most intimate revelations. Then, without meaning to, I had an inspiration, "I'm going to see Father Florida."

I had muttered that, talking to myself. Since the main characters were not talking, nor was Isabel, I preferred being informed by a perfidious yet intelligent man rather than subjecting myself to wild rumors which were certainly spreading all over—rumors I had been fleeing ever since my return to La Paz.

"Please, not him! " Isabel exclaimed.

She had uttered that in such fearful tones that she then had to explain.

"Bah! I'm used to his schemes."

"All this happened because of him."

Having said that, Isabel looked at me reproachfully, as though, by my tactics, I had forced her to surrender a very important piece of information.

"We often exaggerate the extent of Father Florida's schemes," I coldly observed.

"Judge for yourself."

She began a tale which was now unrestrained, now reticent: "First of all, you're the one who brought Jaime and Camilla together. As a result, Father Florida is terribly jealous of you."

"Really?"

"You're not going to tell me that you didn't know?"

Did I know? I perhaps had suspected it before, but I had long since forgotten about it, having scarcely thought about Father Florida over the past few months.

"He's jealous of the influence you have first over Jaime, then over Camilla. The meeting of these two people that you arranged seemed like the end of everything to him. Your absence raised his hopes greatly again. He came here several times."

"But I thought that Camilla was not very anxious to see him."

She hesitated for a second.

"He told her that she had to marry Jaime."

It was irritation, more than disgust, that I felt. It's more irritating than disgusting to see the few beautiful moments of life spoiled by such tedious, subversive tactics. I recognized the Jesuit's plan immediately and his political interest. Yet between Jaime and Camilla it was a question of something deeper than politics, or rather of that deep and unusual feeling for politics which is akin to poetry, music and, who knows, perhaps to the highest form of religion.

"Sure," I snapped disdainfully. "Florida wanted to bring Jaime closer to the nobles by compromising him within one of their families."

Isabel thought that I was pretending to be indifferent.

"He also wanted to tear Jaime away from Conchita's influence," she added half seriously.

Without paying any attention, I went on, "Bah! But in your family there's Doctor Belmez whose politics are completely different."

She answered me without thinking, "Well! It just so happens that Belmez seemed to have an understanding with Florida."

This sudden bit of information caught me by surprise. After a while, I said to myself that I was wrong to be amazed. These two sinister forces, the Jesuits and Freemasons, must have often worked together in the same confused conspiracies. I also remembered Jaime's statement in the beginning—"The Masons and the Jesuits have never been able to do more than acknowledge events after the fact." Two dark and ineffectual forces, but two exciting and debilitating shadows, creating a vile and ridiculous atmosphere around noble deeds. Yet, after all, was this true—what Isabel was confiding in me like this? She wasn't aware of its importance.

"You're not going to tell me that Camilla was involved in all those intrigues?"

Isabel remained silent for a moment. Ever since the first of our conversation she had shown a bitterness which I had at times sensed in her, but which I had never seen rise up into her voice and eyes.

"Not at first."

Once again she was seeing what she didn't want me to see completely or what she wished she hadn't seen. I looked for a way to approach her.

"I assume that Jaime suspected that these intrigues existed or was warned about them and took offense. ... But that doesn't explain the scene in the palace. ... He probably wanted to remind himself only of what had been done or said against Conception."

I whispered to myself, "The disappointment he experienced with Camilla drove him back to Conception and he wanted to avenge her for what he had started to do against her."

Isabel remained silent. I was suddenly disheartened by this extortion of personal secrets I had fallen into and I decided to leave. By thinking matters over, I would undoubtedly fit all the pieces of the puzzle together.

But, as I was getting up, Camilla entered. She recoiled with displeasure, catching us by surprise and guessing what sort of revelations were being exchanged. If she had come to her sister's room, however, it was because she knew that I was there. She had finally given in to the urge to see me. In her open manner, she candidly admitted it on the spot.

"Felipe, I'm sorry that I didn't let you see me. Forgive me. I was going to send for you. Come to my room. Isabel, excuse me, I need him very much."

Isabel yielded as usual and I found myself again in the sitting room hanging over the precipice, where I hadn't been for a long while and where life had flowed irreparably on. The grand piano was there, silent, and flowers were sitting forlornly on the tables, between the books.

Camilla didn't try to hide a profound distress that she displayed with a noble serenity. She had asked me to sit down, then had remained silent, almost stunned. Her features were a little sunken and her pale complexion had fewer warm highlights.

After a long pause, I brought myself to say to her, "Was I wrong to let you meet the most energetic man in this country?" She gave a start, followed by a moan.

"No, Felipe, no."

Then she began to cry.

"Camilla, I don't know anything about what happened. But I can tell you one thing—if you had only shown yourself to Jaime just as you are, he couldn't have resisted you."

I bit my tongue for I was admitting a little cavalierly that Camilla was in love and that perhaps Jaime had refused her love. My instincts had spoken out a little quickly. But she was neither offended nor did she deny it.

She began to study me as though she had never seen me or had never thought of looking at me.

"Felipe, how you love Jaime!"

"I've proved it."

My love for Jaime was made of action. To love him had meant to do so. Suddenly, today, I was thinking that to love him would still mean defending him against everything that sought to destroy him. But did I love his soul? I was not familiar with it and it surprised me at every turn. My action had loved his action, as, between two lovers, passion loves passion.

"But are you willing to give your life for him?"

"I am bound to him in life as well as in death."

I thought about Don Benito. No one in Bolivia knew how Don Benito had died, although Jaime was accused of this in the most haphazard way. The captain and the men who had gone with us were trustworthy. Yes, trustworthy—trustworthy men do exist—soldiers. Agreda disdained betrayal as a civilian entanglement.

"Then, I can't talk to you since you would have to repeat everything to him."

"Jaime would be furious with me if I didn't show respect in his presence for the secrets of someone's heart, at least a heart such as yours."

She studied me at length with such a violent display of gratitude that I gauged at once the great love she had for Jaime.

"I am going to do something crazy, Felipe. I am going to tell you a secret that a woman should tell to no man, not even the one she loves more than anything and not even to her confessor—especially not to him."

"Be careful, Camilla. Wait. Put this off until later. You're still suffering from yesterday's emotional shock. I value your friendship and I wouldn't want you, afterward, to avoid me with horror, having become the bearer of a secret."

"No, you have nothing to fear, Felipe. I'll never be cowardly. But there is only one man and a man who loves Jaime who can explain something horrible to me that I don't understand. And this is killing me."

Again Camilla was crying—she was sobbing. That gave me a breathing spell which I was relieved to get.

"After you went away," she began abruptly, "we had a few days to ourselves. Only a few days but for which I would give my whole life."

I have learned since then that the most gifted individuals thus have only a brief refuge in the midst of life.

"Jaime, in one instant, gave me everything I had dreamed of and much more. He confided in me, he gave himself to me. He told me everything there was in his soul. He had never told this to anyone and had never told it to himself. That evening, he fell to his knees and told me that he knew who he was because of me—that he was discovering himself. He was beside himself."

She stopped, stifled by the memory and gasping for breath. I imagined the scene at the very spot where it had taken place. The power of suggestion was as terrible for me as it was for her.

"He was shaken by the compulsion that had suddenly made him talk and he told me he loved me. As for me, I had loved him since that first day, Felipe, and I marveled at his simplicity, at the generosity of his heart. The only answer I could give was that my heart was fully his. The next two days, we lived in—"

I listened with all the sensitivity and religion of my being. All that was true and, in any event, it had taken place. After all, what happened later was of little importance. The pairing of human beings lasts no longer than a flash of lightning, like that of animals and gods.

"But after that—"

"Stop for a moment, Camilla," I exclaimed. "You're well aware that what you just told me is what counts. No matter what happens next, you are both forever blessed. You have belonged to one another."

"Ah, Felipe."

A terrible convulsion shook her. Some sort of regret or remorse was tearing at her. She looked at me again as though she were seeing me for the first time and said slowly, adopting a very intimate tone all of a sudden, "This is where I confide in you, Felipe, because I know that you belong to him. Ah, I envy your belonging to him in this way. Do you know why I'm going to talk to you?"

She gave me a searching look that was concerned with nothing but me.

"Because Father Florida told me he was sure that you killed Don Benito out of love for Jaime."

A ghastly shiver went through me. Father Florida had touched my soul with his filthy hand and I swore to myself I would kill him. Meanwhile, I was also extremely angry at Camilla. She noticed this but she was too excited to care.

"What you did then is what I would have liked to have done myself," she said with a passion which immediately reconciled me with her ... "Well, Felipe, those first days, Jaime didn't touch me. You understand, our love was so strong."

She fell silent again for a long while. She was no longer crying and her eyes were now dry. Henceforth, for me, there was nothing left for her to say. I could well imagine what had happened. With profound insight, I said to myself, "Ah, of course, I know Jaime's soul well since I can feel everything. Unfortunately!"

My knowledgeable expression did not go unnoticed by Camilla who, grabbing my arm, shouted furiously, "You seem to understand already what I haven't told you yet. Is it so easy then to understand what I don't understand?"

I lowered my head.

"One day, Jaime came back to see me, but later than usual. When he entered, I saw that he had changed. I was afraid, very afraid, but only for a second since I was so very happy he was there. He told me with a harsh rapidity, 'I didn't want to come, I didn't want to come any more. We should leave things the way they are.' I understood his noble thought and, for a moment, I shared it in a state of ecstasy which even surpassed everything I had felt until then. But I loved him, I loved him in every possible way."

She stopped again.

"I loved his body just as passionately as his soul," she tossed out while raising her head in a magnificent gesture. "I was now hungry to be his. He had already noticed this and that is why he moved away from me. In a voice that seemed dreadful to me, he said, 'I'm leaving.' Then, suddenly, I thought about Conchita."

She looked at me with a furious insistence.

"Everything I'm telling you is pointless, and you're not worthy of my confidence if you don't believe this—that I had never thought for a second about Conchita since you brought Jaime to my house the first time ... To me, Jaime seemed above that."

I agreed soberly.

"Then I gave in and threw myself on this sofa," she told me as she pointed an impossibly cruel finger at a piece of furniture behind me, "and all the sorrow of life left my body. Then—"

She lowered her head in deep shame.

"Then he came and took me, and he left."

Silence. Silence. Again silence fell in the music room and I wished that it might always be so enshrouded. Why build houses over an abyss? And why had we come from Cochabamba to La Paz? And why had I wanted to stir people's souls? She was suffering, she was suffering so much! The silence lasted a very long time and it did us no good.

She threw herself upon me again with an angry plea. In this manner her pride reappeared.

"But why on earth don't you talk to me? You're on his side. Does that make you against me? Why did he leave me? I'm pretty, aren't I? I abandoned myself to him as no other woman has ever done nor will ever do. And he loved me, he loved me! I swear to you on Christ's head, Felipe, that he loved me as much as a man can love. What happened then? But tell me since you know!"

Compassion is not my strong point and a feeling so vulgar toward an individual who encompassed such great strength was out of the question. I began to get angry, somewhat like her. I shrugged my shoulders.

"Camilla, why are you questioning me? You must have a reason. It's impossible for you not to have a reason. You most likely want me to know about it. But if you want to free yourself of one of your anxieties, you have to state that reason yourself so you can face up to it."

She scrutinized me with surprise, suspicion and uneasiness.

"He loves me but he believes that he isn't supposed to love me."

"But why?"

"It isn't Conchita—I'm refined and he's afraid of my refinement."

That reason did not seem to me to be the real one. I wasn't expecting Camilla to give me the real one. Giving it to me, if she had been conscious of it, would have doubtlessly meant at that time depriving herself of life itself. But, to my surprise, the reason she mentioned seemed nonetheless true and would be added to the truth of the other that I would not discuss.

Camilla had noticed my surprise.

"What—that's not what you think? Tell me, please, tell me!"

She felt like ripping me apart in order to drag from my carcass whatever would hurt her the most but also that which she could use to devise some means of salvation. At that moment she loathed my ugliness that blended scandalously in her eyes with the enigma of Jaime's virility and beauty.

I was becoming a tempting source of confusion for her mind, and so I tenaciously forced myself not to look at her for a long time in order to interrupt the annoying and dangerous attraction which existed between the two of us.

"No, I think," I murmured, "that you said what was essential in a guarded fashion. Jaime is not in Bolivia to seek pleasure but to act."

"But I understand that! When he was at my feet, I raised him up to tell him that—most of all. In an instant, I stripped myself of everything that wasn't suited for him."

I shook my head as gently as possible, although deep within me I was irritated.

"No, Camilla, people don't change. You are everything he wants to shun. You are the exquisite and delicious diversion of life and he is the spring that will wind itself until it snaps."

She broke into an almost exultant laughter.

"That's just talk, all that. I'm a woman and I'm as capable as any other woman of serving the man I love."

"Not everyone can be a servant."

"There are slaves that degrade their masters, like Conchita."

"Conchita is the absence of women in Jaime's life."

I was surprised at everything I had just said. To be sure, this conversation was leading me to acknowledge an idea that was different from the one I had first had in mind.

Here is the substance of that thought which had first flashed through me: "Jaime cannot love Camilla's body which is too pure. He is afraid of that purity which by contrast condemns in his eyes the infamy of Conchita. He has always suffered from the dancer's irreparable prostitution. He was jealous, beyond jealousy, for the man who is the most prone to jealousy sees the folly of losing his blood through the thousand wounds of a whore. He is horrified at the thought of his body, sullied by Conchita, being joined to Camilla's pure body. Even though Camilla may have had lovers, they didn't affect her. He fled from this thought that was burning inside him.

"Would Camilla be able to cure him? Yes, perhaps, if I were to become very slowly and over a long period of time the one who guided that untrained sensibility.

"Untrained. I look into those eyes which question and don't understand. In all likelihood, at the pinnacle of happiness, she remained innocently unresponsive in the arms of that handsome beast, of that rough and austere trooper who never seems to have made himself the master of Conchita's body. I have always suspected there was a quality in Jaime's manhood that separated him from women. That stallion is the opposite of a ladies' man.

"I know all these things myself, the hideous one who, over the murmuring of my guitar, hears women whisper the secrets of their trade in dance halls."

That was what my initial thought had been. Now, I told myself it was accurate and not worth a thing. Conchita, together with her body, was available to all—the very picture of a soldier and leader's destiny: Jaime, as devoted to Bolivia as Conchita was to the Bolivians, could not let himself be ashamed of Conchita's body.

Therefore, in order to explain this withdrawal by Jaime, it was necessary to consider in turn what Camilla had said: she was life at its finest, the life of the nobles. However, Jaime was there so that something might spring forth in the midst of that delicate life, something coarse and agonizing—something hostile.

With a violent abruptness, Camilla again left her own thoughts only to find that they paralleled mine.

"I know what you're thinking," she exclaimed, "that Jaime belongs to the people and I belong to the nobility. But through me he could surely blend the people with the nobility. As a result, he would truly succeed in forming the highest bond which is the justification of a Protector. He would no longer be the people nor the nobility, he would be both the people and the nobility—he would be the nation."

"No," I retorted with a passionate and quick violence which left us both very surprised. "You could be instrumental to this union only if you were able to create it within yourself first of all. You will never be able to do that. You will never belong to anything except your social class, in spite of your music and books."

It was a shock. My entire relationship, all my plans concerning her came tumbling down. Everything was over between Camilla and me. I was an enemy.

She looked at me with astonishment and rage but also with the sincerity and humility of her immense grief.

"Why did you bring him to me, then?" she uttered with the self-control that a speaker gets from the certainty of going right to the heart of the matter.

I was stunned.

Those words opened up depths into which I gazed with fright. Hadn't I desired this union for narrowly personal reasons, in order to rid myself of my yearning for Camilla? Wasn't I still using Jaime to fulfill my impossible desires—desire for power, for women? Impossible desires because of my theologian's detachment or my deep-seated infirmity.

Hadn't I secretly desired this marriage between the people and the nobility? Wasn't it because of Father Florida's unconscionable meddling that I didn't want this any longer?

"You haven't answered," she continued with a dark and ominous suspicion and accusation.

"I don't know any longer," I confessed. "All of a sudden, I find what you've told me very disturbing. I'm going to think it over and we'll talk about this later."

She shrugged her shoulders more from weariness than from disdain. She let me leave.

V

In La Paz some were saying that Jaime had raped Camilla, that Conception, having returned from the country, had demanded that Camilla be humiliated a second time and that he had willingly obliged her, while others were saying that Camilla had seduced Jaime, but that Jaime, quaking in front of Conception, had been forced to get back in harness and guarantee her satisfaction. The nobles were saying that Jaime had dishonored a Bolivian family and that nothing was sacred to him. The Agreda horsemen and the people believed that Jaime had exercised his right as a man. There was a lot of vague unrest. All in all, everyone was frightened and disconcerted. I sensed that some emissaries were beginning to work that uncertain clay and perhaps with hands even more uncertain. Father Florida, however, had to know what he wanted. It was henceforth impossible for me to see him because I could not have hidden my hate from him and I did not want to think about anything except how to do him in. But I had to find out what his intentions were. For me, he was from now on Jaime's major enemy with whom I would have to fight it out sooner or later.

I came to pay my respects to Jaime. He greeted me late at night in his study where in a corner I could still see Don Benito with a cigar. Conception was there, sprawled in an armchair and smoking.

"You danced marvelously," I said.

"And without you," she sneered.

"The guitarist was top-notch."

"You don't want to make me dance any more."

"I was gone."

"A lot of things happened while you were gone. You meddle in things and then you leave."

Her voice had grown harsh. Jaime said nothing. He was dreaming in front of a map of South America. He had stopped smoking since coming to power.

"Men and women," I soberly answered Conception, "do only what they have to do."

Standing in front of the map, Jaime was an impressive sight. After all, Jaime would have been Jaime without me. What kind of vanity did I have? The type of vanity which also inhabited Florida.

Conception tried for a long time to irritate me until Jaime said, "Go to bed. I have to talk to Felipe."

I noticed there was an indifference in his voice. She gave him a dirty look but didn't have to be told twice.

When she had left, he remained silent.

"Camilla loves you," I finally said.

He didn't answer.

"She loves you and she's heart-broken. She doesn't understand."

"Do you understand?"

"I think I understand. I think I understand what happened between you but not what happened at the palace."

"Then you haven't understood anything."

"No, I understand, Jaime. She came to provoke you, to force you to transform into a public insult what had only been a private gesture."

"I'm an unattached cavalryman, Felipe. A society woman, as they say, will never meddle in my life."

"She's really just a girl. Didn't you open up your life to that girl, even for a moment?"

"Ah, be quiet!"

He stood up, shoving his armchair violently back.

"That's the trap. A girl, yes, and behind the girl the woman who's preparing all her tricks."

"You had conquered her. She would have been nothing more than a woman in love."

"All of her scheming would have come forth in spite of her."

"Were you afraid of fighting?"

"I have other fights."

He pointed to the map.

"You are no doubt right," I murmured.

"There is no doubt. Don't you know my soul?"

"Ah, Jaime, your best friend will always betray you. I'm not a cavalryman. I can't match your pace."

"Why did you throw that woman under my feet?"

"She's beautiful. Beauty should be yours and Conception always —"

"Conception is nothing. I don't need anything."

"I know, I know. I was guided by frivolity."

"Did you have any political plans like Father Florida?" he snickered.

"So, you know."

"Camilla told me everything without realizing that she was telling me."

He gave a shrewd and bitter smile. A moment later, I grew bolder.

"After all, you could conquer her—besides, you did conquer her—and use her. A man like you can marry a woman and not fear her. That would have worried the nobles a great deal. Florida's scheme would then have turned against him."

He stamped his foot.

"But you don't understand! You never understood anything. Am I here for those little schemes? I am here to conquer the nobles; lift up the Indians and restore the Incan empire."

These words were a clap of thunder. A shameful sweat broke out on my body. What was I compared to him? All my deceitful vanity lay in a heap at his feet. He was there, in front of me, tall and alone. I was shaken by a terrible feeling of remorse, a terrible sense of regret. I was suffering just as Camilla was suffering. He was leaving us behind. He was alone—in total isolation. We despised ourselves and pitied him. I foresaw that pity, the only pity possible—the one we feel for greatness.

After that, we entered into a political discussion. It was the first time I had done so with Jaime. I discovered that his only thought was to attack Chile and gain access to the Pacific—the dream of all Bolivians.

"When I was a lieutenant at Cochabamba, I could think of nothing else."

Once again, I was doubting him. I disgustingly made fun of him in my heart. At Cochabamba, he was living it up and only had vague notions of attacking Chile, from time to time, like any Bolivian who has been drinking.

"But if you want to lead the nation into war, you need control of the entire nation—both the nobles and the people."

"No, I'll be able to move ahead only after conquering the nobles."

I shook my head, weakly, turning everything into weakness.

"After all, you're probably right. After that business yesterday, the nobles will have only one idea—to get even and do away with you."

He looked at me with a harsh irony.

"Thanks to you, I'm beginning the fight under adverse conditions. If you hadn't taken me to see that idiot—"

His voice broke. He loved her. Would he come back to her? Should I urge him in that direction? Self-respect kept me interested in this love affair, but also my pity for her. On the other hand, I admired the pure, austere greatness of Jaime's decision. In the long run, hadn't I felt everything that he had sensed instantly in Camilla's character?

"The people are not unhappy that you seduced Camilla."

He smiled weakly, grotesquely.

"At any rate, you'll have to watch Florida very closely. He's the one who will lead the conspiracy of the nobles against you."

I left, at least happy to have said that.

VI

I had a tacit obligation toward Camilla to let her know what Jaime really felt about her. And so, the next morning, I returned to her lofty home.

As I spoke to her, I could see that she was taken aback. For two days she had been nourishing her illusions and now she was in a state of horrible bewilderment. Her unrequited love became a shameless anger. I saw then how right she had been to tell me that her sophistication was of little consequence in comparison with her passion—and what violence was lurking within this sensitive recluse, interested in music and poetry!

"He's a dog!" she shouted. "He's a half-breed who can't get out of his filth and who loves it and doesn't want anything to change. He's afraid of me because he knows I see all his faults and weaknesses. He can't tolerate any witness. He needs a whore who's just as vulgar as he is. And you—you're too intelligent and one day he'll wring your neck. Besides, he despises and hates you."

"Camilla, shout as much as you like, but it's unfortunate that you're degrading yourself, if only in words."

"In words. I've degraded myself in quite a different way." She was looking at me with excessively wide eyes, something I had already noticed at the palace, and which distorted her handsome mask in an almost unpleasant manner. What's more, she made a wild gesture—she touched her breasts.

"I gave myself to a dog, to the worst kind of dog—to a usurper, to a man who stole our freedom, our dignity. What he did to me, he also did to Bolivia. But this is a grotesque and despicable joke that won't last."

I was deeply grieved and frightened. All the exalted myth that I had created around Camilla's name was coming apart and I wondered if Jaime was indeed responsible for this disaster. There was less strength in Camilla than in Conchita.

I withdrew abruptly, filled with disgust and regret. But in the spacious vestibule of the Bustamentes' house I ran into Isabel who led me to an out-of-the-way room.

She was wondering what I had learned from Camilla and Jaime. In spite of my distress, I returned to my curious ways. It was a question of letting her think I knew everything so I could learn the rest.

"I don't understand why Camilla is degrading herself by being jealous of Conception," I began rather abruptly.

"She's a woman."

"But she wants to be an exception. We all wanted her to be an exception, didn't we, Isabel?"

Isabel trembled. This trembling encouraged me to interrogate her mercilessly.

"You prepared her, it's true, to do herself a lot of harm by accepting and cultivating that exalted idea of herself."

Her eyes confessed to a total understanding.

"But in spite of the good reasons she had—" I insinuated, "because I recognize that she had some good reasons—she shouldn't have turned the discussion toward the subject of Conchita."

Those good reasons—I was indeed hoping that Isabel was finally going to let me know what they were. In fact, she was speaking and at the same time showing what she had never yet done—bitterness and revolt toward her sister.

"You think that Camilla had good reasons. No, I have to admit that in this matter she was crazy."

"Crazy! Crazy?"

"Well, Conchita was very sick and I know from a reliable source that she really almost died."

"So what?" I tossed out haphazardly.

"How can you say 'so what'? It was certainly Jaime's duty to go see her."

I began to suspect something.

"Yes, but–" I bravely insisted.

"If she had just let him go without saying anything! But she told him in no uncertain terms that everything would be over between them if he went to her."

How did she know all that? She had been eavesdropping. This was all becoming trivial, wildly trivial, oh so trivial! Disappointed beyond belief, I became fiendish: "There was more than just that," I stated peremptorily.

"Yes, there was everything she said to him. That was how she lost all her honor."

Therefore, Conception had, in spite of everything, played a decisive role. It was hard for me to believe this and so I shook my head in a knowledgeable way. My acting wasn't very good, perhaps, because suddenly Isabel became suspicious of me. At any rate, he changed the subject.

"Do you believe they'll be enemies forever?"

I nodded my head. But at that moment, one of the married sisters, Augusta, burst into the room, exclaiming, "Camilla is leaving for San Pablo. Come, she's out of her mind. She refuses to stay in La Paz another minute."

Camilla left for that distant estate. The next day, Isabel told me that she was in a state of silent bewilderment–so very frightening to see. Although Camilla's defeat had shaken Isabel to the depths of her soul by suddenly questioning her servitude which was dependent upon the feeling she had had for a long time of her older sister's superiority in all things, she was immediately drawn back to her side out of pity and worry.

"She's going to do something foolish."

"She's going to do us all in," Augusta added, who was there again.

Augusta was the wife of Doctor Belmez and she didn't seem to be without some ulterior motive, saying that in my presence. Isabel seemed to regret what her sister had said.

Forewarned, I went to see Doctor Belmez. I blamed myself for not having done so before, but this large man irritated me with his stare and his fatuous belief in his ability to scrutinize and fascinate me. In my opinion, he seemed to be the last person worthy of being cloaked in enigma. The scheming, which he indeed had to be suspected of, seemed to be the most boring and moralistic drivel. By comparison, Florida seemed the paragon of all spiritual heights and undeniably subtle in conceiving his goals if not his methods for attaining them. A comment by Isabel two days before, however, had greatly interested me. There was a collusion between Belmez and Florida in the plan to have Camilla marry Jaime.

I pretended not to know certain things and I said to him, "I have a great deal of respect for love, and for me it is horrible to think that Father Florida has stuck his nose into your sister-in-law's feelings. Without mentioning that this has brought on a catastrophe."

"Ah! so you think like me that Florida has done everything to prevent this marriage?"

I could not hide my surprise—which, moreover, immediately gave way to disbelief. Just knowing that the idea came from Belmez was enough to make it seem suspicious to me.

"Florida had a political interest in the fact that Jaime would be the prisoner of a family like the Bustamentes."

Belmez shot back, "He could only be hostile to a marriage which seemed useful to you."

I didn't dare admit to anyone that political considerations had been of little importance in my dealings. To admit it would have made me lose all authority in the eyes of those people who had decided once and for all, so it seemed, that I was a dangerous fellow.

"Well, then," I blurted out, "each one hoped later on to benefit from this union."

Belmez approved with that tasteless satisfaction he showed every time that Machiavellianism was being discussed.

"At any rate, doctor, everything has collapsed and it so happens that Camilla is heart-broken."

"That's Jaime's fault as well. He played a very dangerous game in this, really dangerous. That wasn't good politics, not at all good politics, and that may prove to be very costly."

I was struck by the doctor's extremely bitter tone.

"Bah," I said, pretending to be casual, "it was common knowledge for a long time that the nobles were against him. After all, you're probably right, since Florida's maneuver, in any event, was only a dodge to put the Protector in a vulnerable position. You ought to congratulate yourselves—that will force Jaime to move closer to you."

Belmez shook his head in an annoyed, hostile manner. That gave me more and more to think about. There was something in all this that was threatening Jaime. Where was this hostility coming from? I would have to give it some thought.

After leaving Belmez, I increasingly felt the need to be better informed as well as investigate all possible leads. Jaime's police didn't inspire me with confidence—neither as to its ability nor its loyalty—and so I trusted no one but myself.

I went to see Isabel regularly. She had always been friendly to me like her sister, but the latter's absence gave her a freedom that was more advantageous to me than I would have ever hoped. She got an obvious satisfaction from being the dominant figure in the house and, for example, being the object of my attentions. At the same time, she was conscious of that little weakness and let me know it. That girl was inhabited by a fantastic insight into things and now a sort of surprising, humorous mood came over her.

I was indignant that she didn't have any suitors. She was beautiful, as beautiful as Camilla, but with overly refined charms that exposed the arid quality of her soul. There was also a certain disorder in her dress which, more than anything else, revealed her profound despair, generated by the idea that she could only imitate or repeat what Camilla had done and that was all useless and unimpressive. Nevertheless, at that moment she felt tempted to escape this fate and the idea took hold in me to nourish this temptation in a decisive manner.

I had—I don't know why—an ally in Augusta Belmez who was constantly showing how pleased she was at my growing involvement with her sister and herself. One day, taking advantage of being alone for a moment, she confided in me, "Isabel is a lot more perceptive than Camilla, but she wants to see things only through our older sister's eyes. That's the reason why at this time she doesn't perceive the danger that Camilla is facing."

What danger was Camilla facing? I could see that there were numerous comings and goings in the Bustamente house, but I didn't dare appear too curious. Finally, I happened to run across one of the cousins, Roberto, who seemed very unhappy to see me there and scowled at me. Since he had come from the *estancia* where Camilla was staying, I asked him how she was doing, but his surly uneasiness made me suspect something. The two cousins, Manuelito and Roberto, had left La Paz with Camilla and since then had been staying by her side. They had always declared their opposition to Jaime and cursed his presence within the house. Weren't they conspiring? Wasn't that the danger that Camilla was facing?

Meanwhile, I met one of Father Florida's henchmen in town to whom by chance I had shown less aversion than to all those who frequented the seminary. This Luis approached me and made overtures. Although I was very leery of him, I let him have his way. He was a rather handsome young man, who was not in the Church but the legal profession. Being very ambitious, his dealings with Florida seemed less despicable than the others. He tossed off two or three barbs about the Jesuits' obsession with politics. I turned a deaf ear, figuring that Florida had assigned him to spy on me. But, all in all, I didn't discourage him completely.

He finally explained to me that he would like nothing better than to be introduced to the Bustamente family. I cocked an ear, and since I would not say anything, to thank me in advance he began to talk bluntly about the role Father Florida had played in the falling-out between Jaime and Camilla.

"Now there was a great idea—" I proclaimed unctuously, "bring the nobles and the people together. But—"

"But?"

"But—wasn't this Father Florida's idea?"

"You're too clever not to have guessed that he did not want this at any price. Father Florida did everything, I can assure you, to estrange Doña Camilla and Don Jaime."

"That's possible."

"Oh, but it's true! It's sad to say, but the very fact that the relationship had been set up by you made it detestable to him."

"Do you believe it's as bad as all that?"

"Father Florida believes that you are holding the position he should be holding in Bolivia."

"He exaggerates. But aren't you exaggerating yourself the damage he's done?"

"Really, Don Felipe, you know this as well as I."

Underneath the flattery, I sensed the presence of an active curiosity.

"I don't know anything."

"I assumed that Don Jaime's police—"

"I never deal with the police."

I decided to phrase that in such a way that he would be unable to believe it. Bragging about one's true nature to such a person might have proved unfortunate.

"Well," he sighed ironically, "I have to tell you then that Father Florida saw Doña Camilla twice in order to encourage her to get married, but he managed to have himself followed by Don Jaime's police. He also left messages around so that one had to believe there was an organized plot among the nobles, in which Doña Camilla herself was implicated, to link Don Jaime to the fate of the nobles by this marriage."

Isabel had gotten wind of all this, believing that Camilla had truly been implicated in everything, and that was why she was so bitter.

Another bright idea came to me.

"He really outdid himself, your Father Florida, by sending a certain note."

"He sent several."

"Anonymous ones."

"Some anonymous, the others carrying his beautiful signature, on purpose."

"But there was one note in particular."

Young Luis' eyes flashed with greediness.

"I don't know, but tell me quickly!" he exclaimed.

"Well now! If Camilla came to the palace, it's because she received a note. That note was from Father Florida and well phrased."

"My God, that may have been his masterpiece. I would give my doctor of law degree to read it. Do you have it?"

I was going to say stupidly—"no"—but I assumed a knowing air.

"Maybe."

"Ah, if you ever permit me to be your friend, will you show it to me?"

He was forever stooping to ignoble acts, but would raise himself up immediately by means of a spirited, exuberant and lascivious irony, directed at everyone.

I admired the subtlety of Florida's schemes when I was alone.

This young Luis could be very useful to me, and I needed to make friends with him, however much one can befriend such a treacherous species. Instead of looking for a clumsy excuse that she would have seen through, I told Isabel frankly that Luis was anxious to meet her. She had shaken off her traces and she went along with the idea. In a very short time, to my utter surprise, I saw that she was fond of the young man.

I had frequent talks with Luis. His look of increasingly noticeable satisfaction told me a great deal about his progress in Isabel's affections. He was sincerely in love and his gratitude seemed willing to be limitless.

I was careful.

"You're still seeing Father Florida. How do you explain your relations with me and Isabel Bustamente to him?"

"I pretend to be scatter-brained and let him believe that it's all because of love."

"Is it all because of love?"

"No, I want to be of service to you, and to Don Jaime through you. To tell you the whole truth, I believe in the future of Don Jaime and want to be a part of it ... That's why I'm following so closely the conspiracy that's developing."

There had been a conspiracy and he was situated at the very heart of the conspiracy. Isabel had become his mistress with a prompt and calm boldness that completely unnerved me. She didn't hide from him long that Manuelito and Roberto Bustamente had entered into an assassination plot against Jaime. Camilla, who had given herself to Manuelito, was lending a hand, and there was not the slightest doubt about that. From Camilla's *estancia*, messengers would gallop to meet those sent by Father Florida.

This strange young man, Luis, told me that in one fell swoop. He didn't seem bothered in the least by the fact that he was getting his information in the bed of a woman he loved. For the time being, he hadn't obtained anything more specific because Isabel could be alone with him only for short periods of time.

"She's so beautiful that I have a hard time regaining my composure enough to make her talk. She's telling me everything out of sheer love and because she's obsessed with fear. She's convinced that everything will turn out badly and her family will be ruined by it."

"She's the one who's preparing that ruin by not stopping Camilla."

"No, because she and I, dear Don Felipe, are hoping that the Protector will be able to distinguish between the good and the bad in the Bustamente family."

The scoundrel amused me and even charmed me, for all his baseness had been swept away by the ecstatic expression his adventure had given him. He had not the least desire to keep me from knowing that Isabel was demonstrating the most felicitous sensuality. Luis, who had not known her in the presence of Camilla, could not be astonished by this like me. This change did not seem any less one of the joys of my life. It was with personal satisfaction that, while visiting the young woman, I was able to see her mask—which retained the same appearance as before—crack from time to time under the rush of memories and anticipation. I made that secret joy a part of myself with an even greater delight. I derived as great a consolation from such circumstances as from my theological meditations—very infrequent these days—because, for me, not having been initiated into the highest ecstasies, good is as much in God as it is within certain moments of the world, doubtlessly because God's presence therein is furtively perceived. The important thing is to realize that these moments cannot nor must not last.

Isabel's fleeting happiness made me, not without bitterness, feel sorry for Camilla's failure. I began to imagine the emotional state in which Camilla might now be and I pictured the deep pit her love was digging for her hate. Yet, deep in my heart, I welcomed the idea that, for these two powerful creatures, hindered by their very strength, the struggle under way was the only embrace possible.

The time wasn't right for dreaming, although dreams are very useful. I wondered in a perplexed way just how I was supposed to act around Jaime. If I told him what I already knew, he would run the risk —being poorly served by his police—of spoiling everything. But if I kept quiet, I could make him lose time or even make myself look suspicious. I would see him now and then, and he seemed to be increasingly absorbed in his military preparations. He was organizing the army for war with Chile, and in that he demonstrated a devotion, an ardor and a genius that were worthy of my unceasing vigilance.

At that time, I considered taking the bull by the horns and running over to San Pablo to Camilla's *estancia*, in order to lay the very greatness of Jaime before her eyes and explain how she was being untrue to herself by no longer recognizing this greatness.

Since I wasn't completely sure of Luis, I didn't dare discuss this plan openly with him. On second thought, however, I had to agree that, if I could count on Camilla's generosity, I would not escape— deep within this province—from Father Florida or Manuelito Bustamente, Camilla's favorite cousin.

I began to be worried and impatient and to demand precise information from Luis. Weren't his dealings with me just a sly defensive maneuver by Father Florida who wanted to divert my attention in this manner and lull me to sleep? Wasn't I missing the essential point?

I sent out feelers in Belmez's direction. His wife studied me at length with a knowing look. Wasn't she kept informed by her sisters and didn't she tell him about this? The conspiracy of San Pablo might well result in the victory of the nobles—which seemed contrary to the Freemasons' political goals. It is true that Jaime had perhaps not given the latter enough assurances. This was no doubt the reason for

Belmez's bad mood. After all, were he and his sect really so hostile to the nobles?

Was it only for personal ambition that Belmez had wanted Jaime to become a part of the Bustamente family? Wasn't it really to keep lines of communication open from all sides to his sect?

Strange Bustamente family in whom all the nation's strength was building up and dissipating! Was Isabel consciously betraying her sister or did she see no other way to save her except by having the conspiracy fail beforehand? Did she still love her the least little bit? Yes, she was noble-minded.

VII

I was returning home one night, thinking about all these things, when a man came stealthily toward me—a man whom I recognized as one of the Agreda horsemen, having become one of Jaime's bodyguards. His spurs rang out on the pointed cobblestones of my wretched neighborhood. He said to me, "Come with me. Our Jaime is waiting for you."

He led me toward a nearby suburb. In a small street, men and horses were waiting. Jaime was there and said, "You took long enough, Christ Almighty! Mount up, Felipe. Hold tight. We're going to ride all night long."

I stifled a moan and we left.

That wild ride reminded me of another. It didn't seem as cruel to me because, in the meantime, I had gotten used to a horse. Where were we going? The most improbable and contradictory ideas crossed my mind. The terrifying thought came to me at first that we were fleeing, that a conspiracy had broken out against Jaime. But no, there would have been some hint of that beforehand. In La Paz Jaime had considerable means of defense, a large number of trusted men— all from Agreda. Next, I thought that he was being carried away by his love for Camilla, that he was going to meet her. In fact, we were heading toward the north, therefore toward the *estancia* of San Pablo del Desierto. But why did he make me go with him? Out of romantic superstitions? That didn't seem satisfactory to me.

When daybreak came, I noticed that Jaime and the others were in civilian clothes. Jaime had a terribly intense and aloof look. We followed a roundabout trail and took precautions not to be seen. There was a lead horseman and two or three times he gave a signal which made us hide. We finally stopped in a remote spot where other riders were waiting for us with fresh horses. Jaime conferred with their leader, then we ate and drank. No one spoke, and I questioned no one—not even Jaime who didn't look at me and seemed not to notice my presence. I thought we were going to leave again but Jaime said, "Let's get some sleep. We'll leave at nightfall." Everyone bedded down, except the sentries.

I was awakened by the snorting of the horses that were being saddled. The men were checking their weapons. It was then that Jaime said to me, "We're going to Doña Camilla's, where I have something to do. When we get there, you're not to leave me for any reason. Always stay beside me." I began to guess what it was all about and a profound curiosity occupied my entire being.

It was very dark. Only one man went with Jaime and me. I knew him—it was Ignacio, the most famous sharpshooter of the Agreda horsemen. We proceeded very slowly and now and then we met small groups of men on foot with whom we would exchange a signal—a whistle.

All of a sudden, we found ourselves at the entrance to a long, tree-lined lane which the Bustamente sisters had bragged to me about —we were at the *estancia*. Jaime broke into a full gallop and we rushed up to the front of the main house. There were horses and men around. Someone, a rifle in hand, moved forward. Jaime jumped to the ground and called out to him, "Companions of the scapular." He motioned to me to follow him quickly. Ignacio was at his side. The man with the rifle stepped aside as he saluted. We swept through the portal. Servants hurried toward us. Jaime pushed them aside and we found ourselves in a large room. There were some ten men present and Camilla.

They seemed dumbfounded, crushed at the sight of us. They all turned pale as well as Camilla herself. Her eyes were open wide—a trait I was now familiar with.

Ignacio closed the door behind us. Jaime removed his hat with a sweeping gesture and said loudly, "Doña Camilla, I've come from La Paz to pay you a visit. I'm happy to find all these gentlemen gathered here."

Manuelito Bustamente was standing next to her. Suddenly, he started to draw his pistol. Ignacio quickly had one in each hand and Jaime as well. I drew the one they had given me.

"It's no use," exclaimed Jaime, "we've got you covered. Take his gun, Felipe."

While Jaime and Ignacio's four pistols held them at bay, I went around to each gun belt. They were all armed and I stacked a small arsenal in the armchair that Jaime pointed out to me.

As I disarmed them, I recognized them. They were the gilded youth of Bolivia. They all seemed completely dejected and had a sickly appearance. Only Manuelito showed more anger than terror. He would glare furiously at Jaime, then at Camilla. She was making an intense effort to regain her composure with her eyes fixed on Jaime. She finally said in a choked voice, "You're still cheating, Excellency."

"I just know the game which amateurs like yourselves were very wrong to want to play. Sit down, all of you."

They had all instinctively piled into a corner of the room where there were almost no chairs. Instead of sitting, they slumped to the floor.

"A chair for Manuelito," Jaime shouted and sent the object sliding over the pretty floor toward him with the toe of his boot. "And you, Doña Camilla, over on this side."

She slipped onto a couch where she then sat stiffly erect.

"You had all agreed to kill me. That was to take place on my next trip to the Chilean border. You lost time and you went about it in the wrong way. I could kill all of you like dogs at this very moment. But that's not my intention. Bolivia will soon need all of its young men for combat. I suggest that you enlist in our new cavalry regiment—except Manuelito."

A sense of relief relaxed the huddled bodies. Jaime looked at Manuelito, then at Camilla.

"You, Manuelito, you're not the real leader, but you seem to be. I want to deal with you differently. We are going to fight, both of us."

Manuelito was drenched with perspiration, but he straightened up rather well. Jaime looked at Camilla.

"You're cheating again, Excellency," she exclaimed in a firmer tone of voice. "You want to kill him because he's my lover."

Jaime trembled but turned back to Manuelito.

"We're going to fight with pistols. Right here. This room is large enough. All these gentlemen will bear witness to the fairness of the fight."

"You might as well kill me the way you killed Don Benito," Manuelito grumbled.

Jaime's expression grew tense like my own.

"No one has ever known who killed Don Benito," Jaime announced in a steady voice.

"All Bolivia knows who!" Camilla shouted, without thinking of me.

"Bolivia knows that it will always need a leader and the leader it now has will open the way to the Pacific."

Jaime looked at the young men sitting on the ground, who were trembling under his gaze.

"All right, do you want to fight?" Jaime asked.

"Yes, if the conditions are right."

"Your brother Roberto and Felipe will get the pistols ready. They will give them to us here, in the middle of the room. We'll turn our backs and walk toward opposite ends of the room. At a given signal, we'll turn around. Now, if you turn around beforehand, Ignacio will cut you down. Understood?"

"Yes."

Jaime had all the young men get behind Camilla's sofa, as if behind a wall. She had become completely rigid.

The preparations were made. I had a lot of trouble in repressing a tremble. Roberto was also trying very hard to keep himself under control. We dropped a pistol but Jaime only shrugged his shoulders, taking a savage pleasure in his steadiness.

Manuelito had settled down considerably. He had calmly and carefully wiped his sweaty hands with a handkerchief. Just as the first positions were to be taken, Camilla shouted from within the group,

"Manuelito, you're a brave person and I love you! This man is a usurper and a murderer!"

Jaime replied indifferently, "Quiet! He'll vindicate himself if he can."

Ignacio was showing a deep satisfaction. He was looking at the pretty room, the pretty woman, and all these rich young men with a silent, twisted smile on his lips.

"Let's go," Jaime said.

The two men received their weapons from our hands. We went to join the others behind the couch. I looked at Camilla who had not once looked at me.

"Ignacio, give the commands. We'll walk up to the wall. When we're right at the wall, you'll shout, 'Go!' "

That was done. Naturally, Manuelito fell with a bullet between the eyes. Camilla screamed loudly.

The two pistol shots acted like a signal through the open windows. Jaime's men, who were near the house, rushed forward and invaded it. Jaime kept them out of the room.

He had Manuelito placed on the sofa and said to the young men, "You can take your horses and return to La Paz. But I think you'll want to sit up with your friend."

He sent for the Bustamentes' house manager and ordered him to turn the room into a mortuary chapel. He picked out two of his officers to present arms, saber in hand.

Doña Camilla had withdrawn as though dead. Jaime left the house and camped outside with his men around large fires. They slaughtered some of the *estancias* sheep and had them roasted. After the meal, they sang around the fires.

I thought about Camilla in her room and I reflected on what had happened.

First of all, my investigation into the conspiracy had served no useful purpose. My idea to protect Jaime was a selfish one—he needed no help to protect himself. Then, Camilla had become her cousin's mistress in order to better insure her revenge. I had therefore made her a mortal enemy of Jaime and I had put Jaime in a difficult situation which he had resolved tonight with his savage elegance. I was no good at protecting him but I was eternally good at dipping his hands in blood.

Propped on an elbow, I watched him sleep. Turning my gaze back to the fire, I saw in the writhing flames the amazing and intermeshing configurations of destiny. I was bound to this man by much narrower and special bonds than I had first imagined. It was really a life-long commitment.

The next day, Jaime asked to see Doña Camilla who refused, but he forced his way into her room. He stationed me in front of the door and closed himself in with her for a long time.

When he came out, he quickly mounted his horse and we started back toward La Paz. As he was leaving, I had avidly searched Jaime's face but it was inexorably closed. We went back at the same pace as when we came.

PART III

THE REVOLT OF THE INDIANS

I

The most unexpected and disastrous event had swept down on Jaime.

Suddenly, a terrifying revolt–similar to the two or three that break out every century in Bolivia–had stirred up the Indians in three provinces. The Indians endure everything and then, one day, they turn everything upside down. An absolute frenzy takes hold of them. They run together as a mob and kill and burn. They kill anyone who is their master–men, women, children, old people. They slaughter animals, they burn and tear down houses. They wind up projecting the desolation in their hearts all over the country. The terrible Indian chant, mournful and piercing, shows what it is–a knife that enters the bowels, a fingernail that scratches your eyes out, a tooth that tears off a breast or sex organ, a look that ignites a harvest.

All this was happening under Jaime's leadership–a man who loved the Indians, who dreamed of lifting them out of their misery, who perhaps had some Indian blood.

Jaime had rushed from La Paz with the Agreda regiment. A few days later, he had sent for me with the following note: "Come. I kill, I suffer and I would like to die." As I hurried toward Jaime's headquarters, I saw the results of the Indian's anger. Death had struck the villages where everything was burned to a crisp. Ashes upon ashes. There were only shrunken mummies of men and animals left–fetuses of nothingness among the ruins which were the futureless wailings of chaos. Nature, with the primitive forms of its grasses and plants, was quickly covering over, in the haste of our tropical countries, that other blossoming which had come from its breast and had tried to free itself–the houses of men and all their strange machinations.

I had found a devastated man who was suffocating from a loathsome inner anger, an anger he was clinging to for fear that, should he let go, he would find nothing but despair and immobility.

He greeted me in front of his officers with his usual aloofness, but once alone with me, he let me see all his grief. He paced back and forth, wringing his hands.

"How could this have happened? Everything I've done in office was designed to improve the lot of those miserable people. Is that what tempted them? I am forced to suppress them. One can't reason with madness. They're crazy, they're destroying everything, they're destroying themselves. What I have to do here is horrible."

He stopped to look at me. He was trembling like a horse before something in the road that frightens it and will make it bolt. He continued in a blind rage, "Now they will always hate me. My entire dream to use their support has been shattered. They wanted that—they understood that they could hurt me there. Who wanted that? Those filthy dogs! I'll find them, I'll accuse them in front of the entire nation, I'll punish them horribly. I'll draw their blood drop by drop. But who is it? You have to find them for me."

I was very moved by the sight of this man. With all my strength, I wanted to relieve and gratify him. I had only one thought which briefly did me some good—arrest, torture Florida, make him talk, make him confess all his hatred, all his poison. Everything was being done by him and his nobles. But immediately after, that idea seemed limited and disappointing.

"Florida's surely the one who organized all this business. Have you arrested him?"

"No. And I'm not going to arrest him."

"Why?"

"Because things are not so simple, because he's not alone. I've had him watched for a long time. The nobles are the first to be affected by the revolt. I don't believe they are all mixed up in it. If certain people were involved and Florida as well, that would have been done very cautiously. It will be very difficult and very drawn out to learn how it started, unless we have some luck. ... You despise Florida, but that's no reason to think he's the only one in Bolivian politics."

Jaime had sent out into the rebellious provinces a series of independent columns which proceeded according to a very simple but deliberate plan. He moved about in all directions with astonishing speed and returned again and again to his headquarters and La Paz in order to maintain a broad perspective. He gave me the wherewithal to travel–myself as well–all over the country and to view everything as a private citizen. Above all, what I was to inquire about was the morale of the general population and the army–and the relationship between the two of them. Inasmuch as I was familiar with the Indians, I was to renew their acquaintance, try to understand the grievances that motivated them and the measures that could settle them down. Yet I also had to identify the chief instigators.

"Why don't you just put me in your secret police?"

"You wouldn't understand, and, not understanding anything, you would feel disgusted and wouldn't be useful. Only you can do what I'm asking you to do."

I accepted and solemnly promised myself to take advantage of my mission in order to do away with Florida. I thought right then of going to see the oldest Indian friend I had, Tamila. He was a sort of sorcerer, well-known among the Indians, who lived in a high valley and who was always at the heart of every rumor.

It was there I had departed from and it was there I was returning. I had taken my oldest rags and was living in among the people. I was covered with lice. I insist upon remembering that even though I could pompously choose to remember only the moral anguish that I was feeling at the time. Life in Tamila's house was unbearable. That dirty and noisy house remained suspended–defying the laws of gravity–on a giddily steep mountain slope. Whenever I would enter or leave, I had to climb out or slide down, in the midst of pigs, fowl and llamas. These animals occupied the inside as well as the outside of the house, but, inside, their numbers were doubled by Tamila's many brats. Yet Tamila was the quietest and most judicious of men. His wife could also be as silent as he.

I had been visiting Tamila for years and yet I didn't know him. I was painfully aware, by his reactions, that I had failed to understand the Indians. Was he a common villager sorcerer? Did he indeed possess ancient and profound secrets? Did he have a decisive power over the Indians? Or was he only a low-level political agent–a go-between for all kinds of schemers? Did he like me or did he put up with me because of financial rewards? Did he think I was sincere with him? Did he think clearly, or was he muddle-headed?

All these questions that I had often asked myself in the past grew crucially important under the present circumstances. He was certainly involved in the revolt and yet he hadn't budged from his district which had been the first to be retaken by Jaime's columns.

I started to besiege him.

"Why did you people revolt?"

"The Indians are unhappy. They would rather die than live."

"But why now?"

"Yesterday or tomorrow—it matters little to a man who wants to die."

In spite of the reticence that events had imposed upon him, even toward an old friend like me, he remembered little by little my past concern for the Indians. He nodded his head.

One day, I ventured the observation, "There are people from La Paz who are connected with this revolt. You know them. Tell me who they are. After that, Don Jaime asks only to forgive. You're not going to let your brothers be massacred. You must know that they will only succeed in increasing their suffering."

"Suffering is nothing for those who live in misery. The Indians are no longer the only ones who suffer now."

He would repeat like a memorized—and despised—lesson that the governors' excessive demands had started everything. In the long run, he admitted, however, that strange people were roaming through the provinces. He had been told about them but he didn't know them. It was hard for him to get to know them. He would try to keep me informed. If I murmured that he was playing games with me, Tamila would not open his mouth again all day long.

Meanwhile, the revolt went on, stopping in one area only to flare up in another, intensifying the repression and being intensified by it. In the distance, I could hear the hoarse moans of Jaime.

II

I would visit headquarters on a somewhat regular basis. One day, while coming out of Jaime's house, I found myself face to face with the Indian guitarist who had accompanied Conception during the famous reception at the palace. Since that time, we had gotten to know each other and he had been very touched by my admiration, by my lack of jealousy. My jealousy was only prevalent in the political arena, against Florida. For several years, people had grown accustomed to thinking of me as someone other than a guitarist, and so Antonio could feel flattered by my friendship as being that of an important person who just happened to be a rather good judge of music.

That day, I found him changed, with a small air of importance I had not seen before. I noticed that he wanted to brag about something and at the same time he was so bothered by it that he was afraid.

"How's Conception doing? Is she in La Paz?"

"No, she's here," he whispered, even more mysterious and vain.

"What's so unusual about that? Jaime sent for her to be with him."

"Jaime has other things to worry about."

He said that without bitterness. He was one of those unusual, very civilized Indians who were not disturbed and rejoicing deep in their hearts over the revolt.

"What do you mean? Tell me. What are you hiding from a friend?"

"It's precisely because you are a friend, Don Felipe, that I wish to speak to you. But it's a very sensitive subject. I need to place a great trust in you because my life is at stake."

He now seemed overcome by fear. He was afraid to speak, afraid of what he had to say.

"I know that Father Florida is your enemy."

"How do you know?"

He smiled.

"Everyone knows and even Conception told me so. Now's the time, Don Felipe, that you must swear not to talk. Even if you are very angry, you must act as though you knew nothing. Well—the other night Father Florida was admitted to His Excellency's quarters and conferred a long time with him."

Anger gripped me, in effect—a white-hot anger. I quickly tried to reason things out: "The nobles are afraid of the way the revolt is progressing—this revolt that they most probably stirred up, some of them at least—and they are coming to terms." I should have been delighted therefore with Florida's action, but jealousy was choking me. Jaime had done that without my help. I forgot that I had always fled his overtures and refused to be completely a part of his advisory staff. What's more, my presence at such an interview would only have intimidated Florida. As a matter of fact, hadn't I played a very controversial role between Camilla and Jaime?

It didn't matter—jealousy ruled me, fear as well.

"What did Florida tell him, Antonio?"

"I don't know. If I knew, I would tell you. I would tell you because I really need you, Don Felipe."

"Speak, trust me. You're a real guitarist—you're the greatest guitarist in Bolivia."

"Thank you, Don Felipe. Coming from you, those words would make me crazy with joy at any other time. But, I have made a big mistake. I don't know if I can—"

"Speak, by the breasts of the Virgin!"

We were standing by Jaime's door when he came out. Seeing him, Antonio seemed terrified and abandoned me on the spot without saying another word. I looked reproachfully at Jaime and walked toward him, driven by a powerful urge. But he was already on his horse and riding away. I stopped and didn't try to flag him down. It was better this way. What would I have said to him in my too personal confusion?

I returned to see Tamila. I was very perturbed, but more determined than ever to use him. I got him to talk about the clergy. What was the role of the priests and bishops in the revolt? Wasn't it necessary to look in their direction to find the emissaries from La Paz?

He always gazed at me with a dull or aloof expression; however, a glimmer of irony filtered through his pupils. I had refused to talk to him openly of Florida, but the next day when I mentioned this name in connection with something else, he looked at me with the same irony as the day before.

I thought I had an explanation for this, a disturbing one, when I saw Antonio slip out of Tamila's house one morning at daybreak and disappear in a flash before my very eyes.

Was everyone against me then? Tamila knew a lot about the situation. He and Antonio were most likely agents for Florida.

As a consolation, I told myself that I had not lost contact with La Paz where I was still counting on Luis' agile mind. He wrote me secretly that he was on an interesting trail but, unfortunately, no revelation followed his promises. He had the bad taste to discuss his love life with me again—the pleasures of his life in the midst of the Bustamente sisters. For me, covered with lice, smelling like corpses and charred wood, everything seemed more and more exasperating.

III

I received a letter from Luis containing something new. I was confused again. Isabel, of whom he was the increasingly satisfied lover, had confided in him that Camilla, far from holding Manuelito's murder against Jaime, had only taken up with her cousin as an instrument of revenge. Yet he had turned out to be as boring in bed as elsewhere and she had willingly given herself again to the assassin the day after the murder behind the door that I was guarding. Since then, she had been seeing him on a farm that was hers and where she was now living in the general vicinity of the fighting.

It was clear then—the party of the nobles was working to move closer to Jaime by way of Camilla and Florida. Camilla must have continued the relationship she had had with Florida at the time of Manuelito's conspiracy. There was no doubt then that she had gone back with the Protector for that purpose. Was she now interested in politics? That exclamation in the palace—"The common people are not suited for palaces"—had a meaning. When the rights of the aristocracy fall, they only fall into female hands. Women are always there to bring ambiguity and fraud back into the deserted palace.

I felt myself besieged by bitter feelings and worries that were so personal I was afraid of misjudging the situation. But it seemed impossible for me not to fear that—under pressure from the problems the Indian revolt was creating for him—Jaime might concede too much to the party of the nobles. I tried to reassure myself—without any success—by imagining that the nobles ought to be truly afraid since they were the ones who were seeing their houses and crops go up in flames, their managers massacred and who were very much in need of Jaime's strong arm.

Should I return to Jaime's headquarters? I would show up empty-handed. I threw myself at Tamila and Luis with furiously humble pleas. I had to have the truth at any price. It was the only way to fight against Florida who, assuredly, was not telling it.

I wrote to Luis and chatted with Tamila; yet ever since I had mentioned Florida to him, he had not said anything to me at all. Not knowing exactly what to do, in desperate need of information, suffering from my isolation and under the impression I was losing contact with everyone, I got the idea to go see Camilla—whose lovers' retreat was only an easy day's ride from Tamila's district. That was a little risky, considering I could meet Jaime there or he could hear about my trip and think it indiscreet. But letting Camilla know ahead of time would take too long and I was impatient.

I found her alone and in surroundings that hardly resembled her house in La Paz or in San Pablo. It was a small farm—completely primitive—as is everything in our country once you leave the relatively few rich homes of La Paz. Camilla seemed to have adjusted to it. It is true that she had arranged a rather pleasant bedroom for herself around a large, elaborately decorated couch. On the white-washed walls, harnesses and weapons were hanging. No piano, no flowers (the area was a barren wasteland), a single book, *The Flowers of Evil* by Charles Baudelaire, which had arrived in Bolivia a short time before. That had come to us from one of our country's diplomats in Rio de Janeiro, who got it from the French representative in the region, Monsieur de Gobineau.

Camilla was very glad to see me because one can love solitude—especially if it is interspersed with love—and yet realize, on someone's arrival, that it weighs heavily on you. I also had my guitar. Camilla was thinner and rather carelessly dressed. As a result, she was much more beautiful. She was especially more beautiful for her entire being was aglow with love and adventure. Wealthy people profit immensely from being ruined or swept up in great upheavals. We played some music first of all, without saying a lot.

"Do you know what happened?" she finally said.

"Yes. But Jaime isn't the one who told me."

"I thought so. Who told you?"

"Unfortunately, rumors."

"Damn! Oh well, too bad."

"Are you happy?"

"I'm alive. Before I wasn't alive."

"Yes, the misunderstanding between Jaime and you was due to the fact that, while already in love, you were still not alive."

I allowed myself that direct observation, but she wasn't offended by it, because she felt like confiding in someone within that solitude. Besides, she had told me so much before in La Paz.

"It's good that Jaime found you again. At this moment, he's in a terrible predicament."

"I know," she said, frowning.

"The people who instigated this revolt are awful criminals and they'll pay dearly for it."

She frowned even more.

"What are you talking about? Did someone instigate this revolt?"

"I don't know, but Jaime will know. ... He already knows, I hope."

"You don't believe the Indians revolted by themselves. They don't need someone to encourage them."

"No, there's something else."

"It's Jaime's fault as well. His governors acted like brutes. Belmez told me that the governor of Oruzo was torturing them. And Jaime let them do it."

I fell silent, sad and displeased. Of course, in one way or another Jaime had been caught in the act but his mistress was too quick to prove that his critics were right.

"What does Belmez think of all that?" I asked.

"He's very upset. So much bloodshed. When you begin shedding blood, you continue to shed blood."

I was indignant. I sensed that Camilla's thoughts were opposed to Jaime. Love, then, had not won her over to Jaime. That shocked and worried me.

We drifted into a rather painful discussion that only increased my uneasiness. How alone Jaime was! How hostile everything was around him and close to him! As for me, how very little I was able to help him! I was sorry for my modesty and indolence. I should never have left him as I had done since he had been in power. I should have risen to his defense. But I was clever only with ideas—or clever with action only during those moments of action which are so intense that it purifies itself and becomes as prompt and simple as thought itself. I didn't dare speak to her openly about Florida and I waited for her to give me some indication about her relationship with the Jesuit. But nothing came forth. Everything she said about politics seemed to be coming from Belmez. I finally was amazed at this and, feeling my way, I exclaimed, "I was told in the past that Belmez and Florida were not such big enemies, and that, at the time of Manuelito's conspiracy, they were meeting at your house."

Camilla gave a shudder and frowned.

"That may have been true but that is certainly no longer the case. Belmez may be a clod but he has a lot more dignity than Florida. And he would certainly never do what Florida is doing right now."

Should I appear not to know? I attempted an ambiguous smile, especially to hide my surprise.

"Yes, Felipe. You had better be careful."

"I think I understand what you mean."

"You understand very well. You must know that Jaime has been seeing Florida. If I were you, I would be more concerned. It really is my fault because I've compromised you in Jaime's eyes."

"Oh, you think so?"

"Yes. Conception is aware that you're the one who intro-uced Jaime to me. She thinks that you're the one who recon-iled me with him. So, it's as much out of hate for you as for me that she brought Florida to see Jaime."

I strained as hard as possible not to show my new astonishment and to maintain a knowledgeable look. Oh, why didn't I let Antonio talk! He undoubtedly had wanted to tell me all this outside the entrance to headquarters.

I had to answer Camilla. I had to keep talking.

"Bah, Jaime is big enough to know who's on his side," I exclaimed.

"Do you think it's normal for him to see Florida who hates you—you, his best friend, his only friend—and who hates me in the bargain."

"He hadn't been seeing him as much as that."

"Oh, whenever Florida gets his foot in the door—"

"Admit that you're sure of only one visit."

"Yes, but that's enough."

"Why would Florida detest you so much?"

"The Manuelito affair had put him in a very awkward position.

She discussed all that with a hint of indifference which did not seem faked. She was motivated but apparently only by immediate, personal concerns.

"Besides," she added, "Florida is jealous of any person who has influence. He thinks I'm too close to my brother-in-law, Belmez."

"In addition to the fact that Belmez is a Mason."

I had never discussed Freemasonry with Camilla who didn't seem to know there was a Mason in her family. Nevertheless, she said sharply, "Belmez doesn't pay much attention to those matters."

"You think so?"

"Of course. You would do well to understand that. He's a better man than we thought."

"I don't understand why he didn't get along better with Jaime."

"There is so much intrigue!"

"Any thinking man ought to understand that Jaime is indispensable to Bolivia and join forces with him at any cost."

She remained silent and that had the most dreadful effect on me.

"What, you love him and you don't think that?"

She made an effort to shake off her listless mood.

"I love him but outside of politics."

"How can you love, outside of politics, a man who is nothing but politics? Weren't you involved in politics with Manuelito? Besides, politics is a part of your family with Belmez."

"Bah, I'm cured of that. Music and love are enough for me."

All that gave me quite a lot to think about.

After the meal, during the night, music returned and we were again brought together by the thought of love. I looked at the beautiful young woman lying on her couch. The way she moved and spoke was different from what I had known. I found her more animal-like, more profound, with a more limited and more precise intelligence. But she was also more diverse, a little tarnished, imperceptibly common. In spite of myself, I thought of Conception.

What could now be her true relationship with Jaime? Was there something more than sensual pleasure which obviously had flared up between them? How much did he trust her? If he did speak openly, it was to an enemy who was now more secretive, more dangerous than in Manuelito's time.

I trembled at the thought of what had been done and what I had wanted in the past. When we want something, we always forget that it means wanting all our lives, with its insidious reversals.

I was a little disgusted, a little jealous. Now that I had spent a few hours with her, Camilla lapsed into a frightful state of distraction which would have humiliated anyone less humble than I. I retired to bed and left the following day at the crack of dawn.

After that visit to Camilla, I had to see Belmez as soon as possible. Besides, I hadn't been to La Paz for a long time. It would perhaps be useful if I saw Luis as well.

My route, however, took me by Tamila's place again. I told him right off the bat, "Tamila, you're not a friend. You're making me waste my time. You have to find me the men I'm looking for. I'll be forced to kill you if you don't help me."

He didn't flinch. But I added, "Aren't some of Dr. Belmez's friends operating in the area?"

He didn't flinch, but his face relaxed. Just as I was leaving, he calmly began to tell me about a man who came from La Paz and, before the revolt, had traveled among the villages, and had now been seen again near the areas where bands of insurgents were moving. He was always on the move, hard to locate. Tamila would try to find out if there might not be a hiding place where I could catch him.

While he spoke in a sullen and indifferent manner, his wife would make drawings in the ashes of the hearth. Her movements were extremely beautiful although she was old and decrepid. Beauty wields great power. Such movements should at least have as much influence as the vibrations of my guitar.

IV

I saw Luis before Belmez. That was necessary and I was lucky I did. Luis was very nice to me. He had still not forgotten that I had put him in the saddle and he didn't even seem to want to forget it. He had acquired an authoritative manner that he softened in my presence.

I told him what I knew and concluded, "As you can see, that dreamy-eyed piano player really has both feet on the ground."

"You must have suspected, when you dreamed about letting her meet Jaime, that something very unusual would happen."

"Devil take me if I expected as much. At any rate, today she is viciously betraying Jaime. While being his mistress, she stays close to the men who have dealt him the terrible blow of this Indian revolt. He's blind and we must open his eyes. But is it still possible? Has he been bewitched? Seeing Florida with him says a lot."

Luis was gazing at me with a touch of irony. Even I had doubts about myself. Everything seemed uncertain and compromised in Jaime's fate and in my own. These thoughts were the reaction to what appeared to be Florida's enormous success—and that was eating my heart out.

Although half-paralyzed by worry, my mind, however, maintained some independence and was astonished to see Luis still committed to my good fortune.

"Isn't Isabel suspicious of your dealings with me?"

His eyes sparkled.

"She isn't supposed to know anything, but doesn't she need to offset her sister?"

I remembered having been present at the birth of Isabel's new feelings. All was treachery and it was natural for Jaime to abandon me.

He saw through my emotional state—which was not difficult.

"How you must suffer from Jaime's woes! Strange things are happening—but, first, I must tell you about my love affair."

All caught up in my selfish depression, I had to force myself to listen to him. For him, everything converged with graceful ease toward a single goal—in one motion he had yearned for the breasts of Isabel Bustamente and Jaime's favor through me. He remained totally happy and confident of the choice he had made.

At last, he got to the main point, once I had told him what I knew.

"You can't imagine how what I am going to tell you confirms what you have heard. Isabel has completely surrendered herself. It's not enough for a woman to prove her love to you, she then has to turn over her family to you—bound hand and foot. Well, not only has Isabel lavished upon me a delicious and very sensitive body, as I have already had the honor of telling you, but she informed me that Beimez plays a much less incidental role in family matters than he seems to. He often has political talks with Camilla."

"Even now?"

"Especially now. Isabel believes that Camilla is spying on Don Jaime for Beimez. What I was burning to tell you is this: for a long time Belmez has been on close terms with Florida. Do you know how? His wife, Augusta, doesn't care for him and is playing around. Nonetheless, since she hates him, she keeps an eye on him to find out all his vices. Having seen him entering a church one evening, she suspected a lovers' tryst and followed him. Not without some surprise, she saw him duck into a confessional booth. Of course, she had always seen this great Mason act like a good Christian, but this latest trait seemed too devout to her. She remained hidden and shortly after her husband's departure, to her surprise it was Father Florida who left the scene. What do you think about that? Isn't that incredible! What do you make of all this?"

Luis was very satisfied with the generally cynical appearance that the world was assuming at that time.

To be sure, I had been very wrong not to have taken this fat Belmez seriously inasmuch as he had the best means of dissimulation —being ridiculous.

"But when did that take place?"

"Oh, a long time ago, before the Indian revolt."

"Now, that doesn't matter any more. Did Augusta tell Isabel about it?"

"Of course. Ever since Isabel has been mine, Augusta has been very close to us because the other sister is pregnant all the time or making love to her husband. Confidentially, Augusta is spying on her husband for me. She's got a crush on her un-official brother-in-law."

"Is he the one she's been cheating on Belmez with?"

"Not yet. I'm too involved with Isabel, but later on—"

"Why is Camilla doing this?"

"The Bustamentes have always had relatives among the Freemasons. Belmez is really the head of the family."

After that, I saw Belmez. I studied him with a now attentive eye, but no matter what I did, I wasn't able to picture him as being more intelligent and more dangerous. He didn't address me with the same attitude as before. He considered me an enemy but didn't show it too much.

"I imagine," I told him point-blank, "that you find this revolt disastrous? And not only for Jaime?"

"Your friend is the one who's truly responsible. He gave the Indians expectations that he wasn't able to fulfill and he created an atmosphere of violence in the country."

He said that to me in a calm, expressionless and almost indifferent voice.

"What? Yet for forty years there has been a succession of revolutions in Bolivia, ever since Independence and the Republic. He's not the one who invented violence and he did bring about peace."

"Is that so?" he said, lowering his eyelids.

"He'll bring it about in spite of schemers who in this instance are criminals."

He kept his eyelids obstinately lowered.

"Do you think, Doctor Belmez, that Father Florida is the one who arranged everything?"

He raised his eyes slowly toward me and answered only this, "The Indians don't need any encouragement to revolt. Torrijos' governors did all the damage."

I had already heard that from the lips of Camilla and Tamila.

"You're very hostile to the Protector," I suggested nervously.

"Oh no, not at all."

"Well then, I hope you're using your influence to help with pacification."

"Oh, when things get out of control—"

"Christ, you don't hide your feelings much. If Jaime knew about them—"

"Bah, Torrijos doesn't listen to you. He doesn't need advisors, just policemen."

"At this moment, he's perhaps right."

We beat around the bush a little, then the doctor wound up looking at me—if not face to face, at least from the corner of his eye.

"You can see, Felipe, where this whole Indian policy of your friend is leading us."

"It was turned against him. It seems, at any rate, that the Masons ought to look favorably on these policies of liberation."

"Things have to be done gently."

"The Masons in France in 1789 weren't gentle."

"On the contrary. They had no other choice."

"Ah, they had surely foreseen that. There is no gentleness in politics—it breeds violence."

His lips tightened. At that moment, I had the feeling he was thinking about the way the Indian revolt was developing—which was something he had not foreseen.

"But," he continued suddenly, "you're no longer concerned with politics and you're letting Florida do everything with your friend."

He added just the right amount of irony so he wouldn't seem to be concealing anything.

"My goodness," I murmured.

"I don't understand your lack of concern. You should try to influence Jaime. The nobles are afraid and are throwing themselves into Jaime's arms but he is also in their arms. He's going to join forces with them and become a reactionary."

He had touched my sore spot.

"Maybe," I admitted.

"You understand, under these conditions, my reticence, my distrust—yes, I admit it—concerning your friend."

So Belmez, who had been close to Florida, was now at loggerheads with him. Everything he had just told me was directed against the Jesuit.

V

I learned that Conception was in La Paz and I went to see her, but she refused to see me. Since she didn't like polite manners and wasn't at all shy, she came to tell me herself.

"You've got a filthy job, guitarist—finding women for your big-shot friends. That's how guitarists in bordellos operate. Go back to your whore, Camilla, and—"

But just then Antonio appeared. Antonio seemed extremely unhappy at what Conchita was saying. Not only did he not hide it, but he proved it by giving her two or three hard slaps. That was what I didn't even consider doing. At the same time I learned that Antonio was Conchita's lover.

When he had forced her to leave, he admitted it to me freely.

"Don Felipe, I've done something foolish, really foolish. That's what I wanted to tell you the other day when His Excellency appeared. Not for anything in the world—womb of Our Lady!—would I have wanted him to see me with you, because you're the only one who can save me when misfortune comes—if, however, you still feel any kindness toward me."

"What misfortune, Antonio?"

"Well—Don Jaime will find out what Conchita is doing with me and he'll have me whipped to death."

I sighed, "You did know it was dangerous."

"But you know how it is, Don Felipe. I work with her. She was willing and she's such a beautiful woman. One would be damned for less. And then—"

"I know what you're going to tell me."

"I'm neither the first nor the last if the devil lets her live."

Suddenly, a thought crossed his mind and he became flustered.

"I realize that you also worked with her. But it's not the same thing. You were Don Jaime's friend—"

He had gotten flustered thinking about my ugliness. I was used to these cutting remarks and for a long time, rather than be angry, I had decided to be understanding, except of course when I was facing vicious little men. Antonio wasn't one of these and I had other things to worry about—Jaime's plight.

"Tell me, Antonio, you didn't tell me it was Conchita who brought Father Florida to see Jaime."

"Ah! I never would have dared tell you for fear that you might hate her and me as well."

"Then why did she do it?"

"First of all, Father Florida has always been her confessor."

"Very interesting."

"You didn't know? Womb of Our Lady! I never should have told you that!"

To put him at ease, I pretended, "Ah! Wait, now I remember. Florida told me himself when we were seeing each other. That began when she came to La Paz with Jaime."

"Yes, I think so."

"So she hates me because of Doña Camilla. I can't blame her for that."

"I realize you understand everything. But there is something else. I would like you to understand this as well so you can forgive her. She loves His Excellency. ... Yes, you know how women are. She thinks that Doña Camilla is bad for Don Jaime and that she's betraying him."

"What?"

We were standing in Conchita's sitting room.

"You have to explain that to me, Antonio. You must suspect that I am not at all close to Doña Camilla. Things didn't happen the way Conchita thinks. I only think about one thing—that no harm come to Don Jaime. Are you for him?"

"Oh, yes! He's a man—that's why I'm so unhappy."

Several emotions made a comical and touching mixture on his somewhat gingerly naive male face.

"Well—speak up!"

"Don't just stand outside. Come in. Wait, I'm going to see where Conchita is."

He disappeared and returned after a long while. I insisted on staying because I had an idea. Was there anything I would not have done for Jaime?

He returned and told me, "She's sorry, she's sorry. But, after all, she liked you and she was hurt by your friendship with Doña Camilla. She said that she is more of an artist than Doña Camilla."

"That's true."

"Come then, Don Felipe, we'll have a talk."

He led me into a sort of unkempt small drawing room where there were glasses, bottles, cigars, and sheets of music.

"I am happy to discuss all this with you at last in a frank manner. Conchita believes that Doña Camilla is working for Doctor Belmez against Jaime. Well, Doctor Belmez is Don Jaime's worst enemy. Conchita knows this."

"How does she know?"

"She knows."

"She can't know this except through Father Florida. But Father Florida and Belmez are in cahoots."

"Oh! Don Felipe, you're behind time. They were, they pretended to be, and they no longer are. That's why Don Jaime saw Florida, because Florida told him_everything that he needed to know about this Doctor Belmez. Rest assured, Don Felipe, Doctor Belmez is the one who's running everything in the Indian affair."

"What exactly do you know about it? Tell me."

"Ah! I don't know. Conchita doesn't know exactly either. She would like very much to know."

"But if all this is true, why doesn't Jaime have Belmez arrested?"

"Probably because he's waiting."

I remained silent a long while. Both Antonio and Conchita were most likely trying to get me to buy Florida's story. The Jesuit was covering all his tracks because he knew that I was after him.

Antonio was observing me with interest.

"Excuse me for asking, but you ought to see Conchita—first, she would like to apologize."

Conchita apologizing—that astonished me.

"I gave her a beating a while ago, you know. She understood that she was wrong."

Although fearing an outrageous scene, I smiled: "Fine. I'll see her."

A second later, Conchita was in the room.

"Felipe, you betrayed me."

We were off to a good start. She was in an old house coat with her customary plunging neckline that ravaged my heart and she pointed a half-smoked cigar at me.

"You betrayed me. No one knows better than you that I am a great dancer."

She looked at Antonio.

"Yes, you realize, Antonio, that Felipe's the one who made me a great dancer. In those days he was as great a guitarist as you. But he also betrayed himself. He chose politics over his guitar."

There was an indestructible friendship in Antonio's eyes as he looked at me.

"Felipe, listen to me. I'm terribly angry at you. You preferred that piano player, that lady, to me, Conchita! But fine ladies whore around more than we do."

She stopped for me to answer. But I didn't answer.

"She proved it—that she was more of a whore than me—and she's still proving it. When I think that she gave herself again to Jaime after he had killed Manuelito. That's immoral. A real woman isn't as immoral as that—"

Antonio interrupted calmly.

"You're getting mixed up, Conchita. You tell me all the time that Camilla took up with His Excellency again because she wanted to betray him and, in fact, avenge Don Manuelito's death."

"Both reasons are true," she said gloomily while taking a deep puff of smoke from her cigar.

"Conchita," I then said coldly, "Antonio has told me something very serious. According to you, Camilla just might be plotting with Belmez."

"I'm positive."

"Florida's the one who wants to make you believe that."

"Florida knows one thing—that without Jaime the Indians would be attacking La Paz. All the churches would be destroyed. And all religion."

She was religious and that was how Florida dominated her. I gently looked at Conchita and said to her, "If everything you say is true and Jaime knows about it, why doesn't he have Belmez arrested?"

Conchita exploded, "Because your Camilla doesn't let him! She's the one who defends Belmez to him. And you—"

"Me? What? I'm not around Jaime all the time. I don't know everything. If you had spoken to me sooner—"

"But are you for Camilla?"

"I'm for Jaime and you know I am. In this matter, you can't blame me for anything. If you hadn't always been cheating on Jaime—"

I looked at Antonio as if to apologize halfway.

"Well!" Conchita shouted. "What do you expect me to do? If I slept only with Jaime, I would kill him. You can't be both a lover and a Protector."

"That's true," Antonio soberly agreed.

"Yes, I know," I murmured. "Let's come back to what matters the most. Florida has denounced Belmez to Jaime. He must have given him some proof."

A wrinkle cut across Conchita's forehead.

Antonio interrupted.

"Ah! Conchita doesn't want to admit that but you know how Florida is. He doesn't want to tell everything. After all, he's happy that Jaime's in a mess."

"He wants to be the only person who can get him out of it."

I felt a flash of joy and Conchita seemed annoyed. She glanced angrily at Antonio who had unmasked Florida. I quickly lowered my eyes.

"How does Camilla betray Jaime, Conchita? Give me some proof. I promise you that I'll use it. What does she do for Belmez?"

"She tells him everything Jaime says and does. That way, Belmez can continue his scheming."

"What scheming?"

"He's the one who's in charge of the Indians."

"Give me proof!"

Conchita and Antonio nodded their heads.

"At any rate, it's very simple," Conchita snickered. "The Indian revolt will never end as long as Camilla is Jaime's mistress."

To me that seemed too simple. I looked at Antonio who didn't seem to be suffering from Conchita's jealousy over Jaime and Camilla. That man was a profound fatalist, a very calm and wise person. His guitar had taught him a great deal as well. His eyes met mine.

"I'm leaving, Conchita," I said. "I thank you for what you've just done for Jaime by talking to me."

"Good-by, Felipe. Come play the guitar with Antonio. That's better than all the rest."

VI

I returned to headquarters and found Jaime in a very bad mood. He blamed me for not getting anywhere. I told him laconically that I was finally on a very serious trail.

"Why don't you look in Belmez's direction?" he asked with a deliberate abruptness, like someone who wants to surprise unguarded emotions on a face.

Deeply affected, I remained silent.

"I don't understand why you don't look in Belmez's direction. I wonder why you're not doing that. There is only one kind of politics—my own."

He had given me a suspicious look that had pierced my heart. Later, while he was feverishly talking to me about the measures he was taking to put an end to the guerrilla attacks, I was even more disheartened by the fact that he was going to dismiss me without having discussed Florida or Camilla.

And that is just what happened. All the way back to Tamila's, I had the most bitter thoughts.

Coming back to my sorcerer, I now understood why he had started to talk only when I had suspected Belmez. Until then, he had undoubtedly been afraid that I might be one of Belmez's friends because of my relations with Camilla. Now, having made up my mind, I would make up his as well. And, in fact: "Did you find Doctor Belmez's agent?"

"Yes," he quickly answered.

"Why didn't you find him for me sooner?"

"I didn't know what you wanted."

"You thought that I was on Belmez's side. But you know I'm Jaime's close friend. Belmez is Jaime's enemy."

"I had been told that—"

"What? Who told you that?"

I studied him closely.

"Florida?"

He didn't finish but it was clear.

Now, everything was clear and all I had to do was act quickly. Yet, in spite of my haste, I lingered with Tamila for a little while longer. Why, in the final analysis, was the sorcerer against Belmez? Did he truly understand that the Indians' welfare was best furthered under Jaime?

"Why are you against Belmez, Tamila?" I asked him with a renewal of my deepest curiosity about his situation.

He remained silent for a long while, but to be sure, he had confidence in me.

"Belmez is a great sorcerer among the Spanish."

"You think so? Perhaps. What then?"

"He knows secrets that the Indians know better than he. He tried to learn them but the Indians say nothing. They are right because we now see that Belmez and the men of his faith do not love the Indians. They pretend to love them, but they love only themselves."

On that final and very useful remark, I left him.

Tamila had given me no more than the name of the village and the house in the village where from time to time the famous messenger he had mentioned would come to dally. In my state of mind, I was in such need of fulfillment and my fear of failure was so great that I felt obligated to carry out the operation almost by myself. I arrived therefore in the specified village with only one man and, disguised as a beggar—I had become the beggar of truth—I was able to observe the house where sooner or later my man had to come. He was pretending to be a traveling salesman for candles and incense. The house belonged to a whore who was neither young nor old, nor beautiful nor ugly; yet she had a sufficient number of clients and I was soon one of these. She looked upon me as rather scraggly and lice-ridden. Yet, inasmuch as I had some money and my guitar, she grew friendlier and told me that a man was crazy about her and traveled miles to come see her every week. He always came in the middle of the night.

"Well, if he shows up in a little while, will you throw me out?"

"Oh sure. He understands that I have other friends but when he's around, there's no one else but him."

I waited, knowing just how I would act at the last minute so the operation would remain a secret. I needed to take this charming candle merchant very much alive.

He didn't come that night and the woman seemed very surprised.

"He hasn't been here for several days. He has never gone this long without visiting me. He will surely come tomorrow night."

She was proud of him and I praised him abundantly. Thus, I came back that evening to keep her company with my guitar. The man who came with me was keeping the horses ready in a neighboring street. Toward midnight, having gotten the wanton creature to drink a little, I gave her a sleeping drug. And so it was that two hours later, when a rider knocked at the door, I was the one who let him in. I had my guitar in my hand and I said to him, pretending to be a little drunk, that the lady of the house, after having been very sick, had gone to sleep.

The man was dreadful and reeked of vice. He tried not to show his disappointment at finding me there, but seeing her hunched over the table, he wanted to wake her. I suggested first that he join me in a drink and the sight of the good wine I had brought gave him other thoughts. He soon went to sleep himself as well.

I bound his hands, tied him to a horse and we left for Jaime's headquarters. Was he hopefully the right catch?

Upon arriving, I left the man in an out-of-the-way place and discreetly notified Jaime who came with only Ignacio, who was an expert in more things than just firing a pistol.

First of all, the man was searched. He had very few papers and they were of no interest. Ignacio began to burn the balls of his feet a little and Jaime asked him quickly, "In what house in La Paz does Doctor Belmez give you his orders?"

The man seemed stunned and terrified but he said nothing.

His feet were burned some more; he groaned and Jaime said to him, "You're afraid of your brothers' revenge, but I am a brother myself and you were deceived."

Jaime whispered something in his ear and the man seemed horribly confused. At the same time, he started to moan seriously and finally he confessed that it was in the Carmelite convent.

"When did you first meet Father Florida there? Did you know him before then?"

"Before what?"

"Before he came to give you orders in this convent as well?" Jaime seemed in control of the situation and I sighed with relief when I realized he was still suspicious of Florida.

Jaime had enough precise facts in hand to force the last bit of information out of the patient. This was done in such a way that, at the end of the interrogation, it was determined that Florida and Belmez had been equally involved in fomenting the Indian revolt, that Belmez had received from Florida the assurance that the governor of Oruzo, who was loyal to the nobles, would deliberately torment the Indians in order to drive them to despair, and that, moreover, Belmez had directed and bribed agitators through the lodges. Many priests were Masons and obeyed him directly without going through Florida.

When it seemed that everything had been extracted from the man, we left, leaving him to Ignacio's last rites.

"You knew a lot about Florida," I murmured in a half-serious, half-joking manner.

Jaime looked at me and smiled teasingly.

"Did that bother you when I saw Florida? You thought I was letting you go."

I blushed like a school girl.

"I see that you found out I was seeing him. It's a long story."

Everything had started with Camilla. He confirmed that, far from holding Manuelito's death against him—whom she didn't love and had taken up with only to spite Jaime—she had surrendered herself again the very morning of the duel and how, since then, she had continued to do so. I caught a glimpse of the truth through Jaime's overly reserved story. Manuelito was the one who had done everything to bring them together. From the moment he had learned that she was her cousin's mistress, he was no longer afraid of her or her purity. And now she herself was a real woman who was making him forget Conception.

"A real woman, Felipe, lying and treacherous. She loves me and hates me at the same time. She always confided in Belmez. He must not have been very enthusiastic about Manuelito's plot because he wants the nobles to be rich but he doesn't want them to be—*powerful,* except a few that he's sure of and just for show. She told me a lot without realizing it."

"Love then was stronger than self-interest?" I exclaimed cheerfully. "How could Belmez tolerate your love affair?"

"He had no other choice and he hoped to take advantage of it."

"When did Florida and Belmez get together again?" I asked.

"Belmez had needed to be informed about Manuelito's plot. Camilla had let him in on the secret. He had asked Camilla to notify Florida that he, Belmez, knew about it and would say nothing. That partial complicity allowed him to move closer to Florida and to ask him later for his support in the Indian revolt."

He looked at me without wavering.

"The revolt grew to such proportions that everyone was frightened. Florida was forced to move closer to me by the terrified nobles. Since he feared Camilla, too close to Belmez, do you know the direction he took?"

"No. … Yes, I do. Through Conchita," I finally said.

"Yes, but how did you know that?"

He frowned.

I told him all the lurid details about the guitarist. He didn't budge.

"I knew. When Florida learned that I had taken up with Camilla again, he had Conchita notified of this and, right away, she saw him. He tried hard to downgrade my idea of Camilla. Then she came to ask me to see him. I didn't hesitate and he calmly sold out Belmez."

"Did he give you any specific facts?"

"He was careful not to, relating to people's names. But he calmly told me about the conversations he had had with him 'in a convent.' My police checked but were unable to tell if that was the place the candle merchant was leaving from. I only guessed it a little while ago.

The rebellion had seriously frightened the priest and, as a result, the suspicion and hate of Masonry had come to the forefront again. With what irony he would say to me, 'I met the Sublime Prince in a convent.' "

"And you don't think there was anything else?"

"Yes, he hates you and he tried to link you with Belmez. He assured me that you were aware of Belmez's entire scheme and were hiding it from me."

He looked at me in a devilishly playful manner.

"Did you believe it?" I asked.

"No. But that was fun having you think that I believed it."

"You really did believe it a little, didn't you?"

"You really did believe that I believed it."

I could judge the agony of doubt and loneliness he had experienced by seeing with what relief he now confided in me once again. He had certainly doubted me and had needed the proof of my innocence that I brought him by delivering Belmez's messenger. Could I hold this against him? Just the same, a great sadness swept over me.

"What are you going to do with Belmez?"

"You'll see," he said very calmly.

I ventured to ask him, "Do you think that Camilla was aware of everything her brother-in-law was doing?"

Nothing could make him lose his quiet composure.

"Of course. She didn't tell me. Thus, she completely betrayed me."

"What? She didn't tell you anything?"

"Absolutely nothing. You must be surprised I put up with that. Yet I like women only when they are prostitutes and betray me."

His face was expressionless.

"There were times when Conchita defended you."

"Bah! Only out of jealousy, for fear of being replaced. And I know she's deceiving me with every stableboy she meets—and not only with this guitarist."

"Are you sure?"

"As much as you are," he retorted. "Coming back to Camilla, I received the confirmation of her betrayal from a source other than the accusations of Conchita and Florida. A certain Luis Agostin, who says he's your friend, came to see me—no doubt urged on by Isabel—and he hinted that I should be leery of Camilla because of Belmez."

I grimaced, as much because Luis had gone over my head as because I was thinking how Isabel actually betrayed Camilla.

"Women are frightening," I murmured.

"They are logical, very realistic. This is every bit Bustamente family politics. The sisters seem to betray each other, whereas, in truth, they offset each other. Isabel had me informed of everything so the entire family would not seem hostile. She surmised that I would put an end to the Indian revolt and, afterward, would be stronger than ever in Bolivia."

"What are you going to do now?"

"You'll see."

I was destined only to watch. I had cut a shabby figure behind the scenes during the Indian revolt. All that human substance—thick and elusive like fish—had both offered itself to me and slipped away in pursuit of its singular whims. I was like a god who was progressively losing control of his creation.

VII

Father Florida was not unaware of that haughty epicureanism which always led the purest minds of the Christian faith as well as other religions to select the most beautiful sites in the world to harbor their scorn and indifference. Therefore, other than the small, very limited terrace which, with its cluster of flowers, was twice the size of his seminary cell in La Paz, he enjoyed a mountain retreat, again very small, yet sitting on a promontory that looked out over the cascade of valleys in the middle of which was suspended La Paz.

The important feature of the retreat was another terrace from which one looked out over an immense country, all of Bolivia, so it seemed. This rest haven was even more laden with flowers than the one in La Paz. Here, the Reverend Father could devote himself with wild abandon to his passion for flowers; here, he could sniff them, inhale them, gorge his mind and heart with their scent; here, he could intoxicate himself, saturate himself at leisure and no doubt, through overexposure, arrive at the unique self-aversion he needed to be completely free of the earth's bonds.

But then, there was ambition. Yet what is it, in a man of this sort, other than the very movement of his ideas in the world?

For one of those unexpected and subtle reasons which now no longer surprised me as in by-gone days, Jaime had brought us together on this exquisite terrace a few days after the death of the candle merchant.

It was at the end of the afternoon, at dusk. We were all seated around a table as if for the most open-minded conversation; nevertheless, Jaime was positioned in such a way that he could observe the faces of Father Florida and Doctor Belmez. But he had to strain to watch Camilla's profile, if he so desired, whereas I was peering directly down into my former friend's face. I was also the one who had the best view of this great country of Bolivia lying at our feet.

We were alone. Guards were discreetly stationed behind clumps of magnolia trees and rose bushes. It goes without saying that none of the participants had come freely and that an official summons had brought them all here.

I did not have my guitar. In my mind, this was a mistake which marred the deeply mysterious atmosphere of this scene that Jaime Torrijos had created—who, for the first time, seemed to be aware of the style of his life and power. Music should accompany such meetings which are both the culmination and conclusion of the struggle. If I had had my guitar, I would have replayed from one moment to the next the main songs that had launched and sustained our entire endeavor and would sustain it again later on. Because in the future there would be greater feats than those which, in the past, had only formed a prelude.

The table was bare with no paper strewn about. At first there was a long silence, a sort of collective meditation. Instead of meditating himself, however, Jaime seemed to be waiting until the others had finished doing so; he then looked at their faces, one after the other, and each one was forced to abandon a few of his masks under this slow scrutiny.

Because of the chill of the high elevation and the paralysis of her feelings, Camilla was wrapped in an Indian cloak I had given her during the trip, for I was the one who had escorted her to the retreat. I hadn't deliberately chosen this cloak but that was all I had been able to find. Its bright colors, however, took on an ambiguous meaning next to the dark suits of Belmez and Florida.

Jaime suddenly opened the debate: "Here is what happened between us," he announced in a deliberate, calm and merciless voice. "Doctor Belmez and Father Florida contributed to my coming to power. Not only did they not use any of the means at their disposal against me, but they even made them available for my use, all things considered. The Church and the Masons let those members of theirs who were so inclined come over to my side. Captain Fernandez, who had been a loyal Mason and enjoyed the highest prestige among the Masons in the army, won a part of the infantry over to my cause. Father Florida, who was the secret advisor of Don Benito, let him act according to his character—very much as though he wanted to be conquered, without, however, depriving himself of the honor of combat.

"Even more than relinquishing his duties, Don Benito wanted to die. That attitude was so strange that one might think it was predetermined. It could be said that Don Benito, having considered the position taken by Father Florida who was his indispensable support, saw a verdict in that and from then on played to lose. But I don't think so. Don Benito was a remarkable man, deeply independent, who could find in his indifference to everything the potential for all sorts of bold ventures. If he had wanted to, he could have done without Father Florida. And in particular, if he had wanted to, he would have had me killed the very first day, the day when he came to review the Agreda regiment. Deciding not to kill me, he had decided that I would kill him. That is what I understood afterward."

This excerpt of Jaime's thoughts and words did not appear to be felt by his listeners as indecent. Camilla was no longer ready to shout, "murderer!", and Father Florida as well as Doctor Belmez had all the blood from the Indian revolt on their hands.

"Why," Jaime continued, "did Florida and Belmez help me?"

While we were waiting for him to begin an explanation and were left hanging by his sudden silence, he went on: "Shortly after I came to power, Florida and Belmez began to plot against me. First of all separately, since Florida has always been the middle man between the Church and the nobles. Although he had first reassured them about me, he then roused their suspicion almost immediately.

"But my policies were reasonable. I didn't grant the advocates of my populism any excessive measures or demands. The measures I took favoring the people did not infringe upon the privileges of the nobles. Father Florida must have been looking for an opportunity to direct the nobles' suspicion against a specific target and transform it into bitterness and hate.

"It's here that Doña Camilla entered the picture."

Jaime let his eyes rest placidly on her, a possessive gaze which confused us all somewhat, including herself.

"There was a great and noble idea in bringing together a Spanish woman and me, the half-breed—because I am a half-breed and starting with me, you will no longer have any other rulers in Bolivia except half-breeds—which is a way of saying that Indian blood will finally triumph."

He had said that harshly, with a savage violence that completely surprised us. He had never said anything to me about that matter, and most of the time I hardly thought about it. Camilla's eyes opened wider. Large white circles extended around the black pupils in which the image of a man once desired and now lost was reflected in miniature. Regret and bitterness were definitive signs of the helplessness of the aristocratic woman whose energy was dissipated by following and overtaking the genius of the common people. Belmez was confused and totally shaken. Father Florida, with an extended shiver, came into possession of a truth he had long suspected from afar. As I said, I was surprised. Once again, I was terrified at being surprised. "I am not a cavalryman, Jaime. I cannot match your pace," I said to myself.

"There was a beautiful and strong idea in this bringing together of a man and a woman, the two halves of the nation. But Father Florida was on the lookout. And it is never without reason that a woman is a well-bred lady, as you say in your affected Parisian chatter. What is a well-bred lady? She's the daughter of a defeated and decapitated aristocracy. In this year 1868, that is more of a fact than ever. That has been the case since 1792. Aristocrats from all over the world are decapitated people who are walking by habit. Here is what your nobles are, Florida; here is what supports the Church. But perhaps the Pope and the cardinals are decapitated people themselves. That will be known one day, in two or three centuries."

Eyes, eyes, eyes! Ah! The eyes around that table! I can see them as if I were still there. The wide-open eyes of Camilla who was snuggly wrapped in her Indian cloak as though to exclude herself from the inevitable. The eyes of Father Florida—enormous and globular—were rolling their particles of fire. His mind was both within and beyond hatred. Belmez's eyes unveiled the depths of hopelessness. In them one could measure the needlessly repeated effort of a school boy, re-reading a lesson he had memorized and realizing, from what the teacher said, that he had never understood its meaning.

As for me, did I recognize in Jaime's words that which I had sometimes whispered to him? Thought having become action, dipped in blood and forged like a weapon of steel, is no longer a part of the thinker.

But how unwise is the man of thought's astonishment at the man of action's ability to learn quickly, for men of action are important only when they are sufficiently men of thought, and men of thought are valuable only because of the embryonic man of action they carry within themselves. I had brought action to Jaime and small indeed would have been my ideas without him. That was what Florida was not forgetting and, at that moment, he gave me a look of soothing flattery.

"I refused Camilla," Jaime continued as though speaking to himself. "The scheme which consisted in having me marry her was too vulgar and too futile. I am not Napoleon—neither the First nor the Third.

"At this point, a secondary question: What did Doña Camilla want? For a while, she was two people: a woman in love and a well-bred lady. The woman in love was hardly concerned about what Father Florida wanted to do with the well-bred lady. But I knew that the two women would be reunited one day, joined against me, in order to defame me in the eyes of the people.

"Moreover, what can I say? They were quickly reunited by the force of circumstances. A humble dancer, who gave me the only thing she had–her body–her spirit having remained in her village ... Doña Camilla Bustamente and Camilla were united as one in forbidding me to go see the sick woman because they wished to insult her and insult me in her."

Jaime, who had recovered his initial calm and for this reason had regained in our eyes an attractive prestige, indulged himself again in violence. He was completely given over, so it seemed, to indignation, to anger. He had suddenly regressed into a lovers' quarrel which he was laying out in front of us. His face was contorted and the looks he gave Camilla were like those you see in street brawls on a hot day.

Camilla was sitting lifelessly and did not have the heart to take advantage of this change of tone.

He continued with a sudden calmness which made us doubt everything. I said "us"–dreadful admission–for I was suddenly thrown in with Florida and Belmez by my emotions.

"That's what aristocracy is–a feeling just as fettered as the feeling of the common people."

That abrupt conclusion both gave me and relieved me of a tremendous headache. He was great, our Jaime–and Florida, covered with all his demons, noticed this with an openly obscene expression that slowly died under Jaime's own.

"Florida was responsible for the event that took place one evening in the palace. He was responsible for the event. Clever people have decreed that I was very inept that evening. These clever people are idiots and weaklings who interpret signs of strength and passion in accordance with the only perspective their weakness permits. I am not inept. I am strong, but I am not only strong, I am a passionate man. There is a passion in me that you will kill only by killing me and you haven't killed me yet. I intend to move through life some more, in a hail of blunders."

"Do you think the first Christians were clever, Florida? Do you think the Puritans and Jacobins, your ancestors, Belmez, were clever?" This was what I shouted. My ideas which had given birth to Jaime's were now racing along with them.

"Therefore," Jaime pursued without blinking, "a futile matrimonial project was transformed into a futile conspiracy– Manuelito's. Manuelito! That is where a woman's weakness can be seen—women as a whole, and no longer just well-bred ladies. Turn your back on a woman, then look at her again and she'll have your caricature in bed with her. Conception with her stableboys was hardly any better than Camilla with her Manuelitos."

He said nothing more on this subject.

"After that, my enemies became more serious. They wanted blood. There is only one occasion when bloodshed is respectable—war. I don't like civil war—me, the soldier. I only make it to get to real war. After all, you like civil war, because you think it will remain within the limits of your puny character."

He was looking at Belmez who was perspiring.

"You're the one, Belmez, who stirred up the Indian revolt. Florida was only half-heartedly involved in it, hoping all the while it would destroy you as well as me. Why did you want the Indian revolt? In this, you were clever and perfidious at will. In the long run, I wanted my administration to depend heavily on the people—that is, on the Indians. You wanted therefore a river of blood to separate me forever from the Indians.

"I wasn't able to foresee and prevent that. I showed myself to be wretchedly inexperienced in this matter. But I won't be caught twice and I will correct that enormous mistake.

"Why did you act, to be sure, as an enemy against me? To answer that, you must look beyond yourselves. The entire Freemason movement acted through you. If the Church defends the nobles, you defend the middle class—the middle class which is still half Spanish or more than half. You saw Indian blood on the rise—which in our country is the blood of an entire people—and you, who are always giving lip service to words like brotherhood—the same as Florida—you wanted to tighten the yoke that Florida's predecessors had placed around the Indians' necks in the past. Because Freemasonry shares with the Church the responsibilities and hypocrisies of private property.

"You took action only at that time when you saw you couldn't attract me into your lair with your sister-in-law. But then you didn't waste any time. You made a mistake, however, a big mistake. You took Florida into your confidence. The Church and Freemasonry are often allies, having been inextricably connected in their beginnings, but they are intermittent allies. Florida wasn't able to resist the temptation of catching you red-handed amid mistakes and abuses. He betrayed you in my presence. Moreover, your wife and your other sister-in-law also betrayed you. They betrayed you because they were women and because they sensed danger for their family. The Bustamente family acted like Bustamentes, which meant that finally they sided with the politics of the nobles who, frightened by the Indian revolt, moved closer to me through Florida.

"And yet the Bustamente family knows the importance of having a foot in the Masons, but only one foot. Camilla betrayed you, perhaps without realizing it, but after all that isn't certain and she betrayed me as well. She betrayed everyone and no one. Like Conception."

Camilla raised her head for the first time. The sarcasm was getting monotonous and wearing thin. No doubt Jaime sensed this for he stopped short: "Those are facts, all that. I now have to sift out the ideas, because facts are governed only by ideas."

I raised my hand to ask to speak.

"I beg your pardon, Excellency, but there is a fact that you didn't mention and which concerns me. That may give these people the impression that you are mistaken about me or that you're favoring me."

"Why were the doctor and Father Florida able to train their guns so rapidly on you? All because of me. How about Camilla herself? Because I was talkative and meddlesome. Because I explained your ideas on the Indians to them, because I was foolish enough to want to convince them."

All the while the Protector had been speaking, I had suddenly and increasingly been struck by this terrifying recurrence: I had invented his enemies. If in the past I had invented the Protector, of late I had invented his enemies. I had forewarned them against him. Jaime had found having a friend with ideas more of a handicap than an advantage.

Jaime, nevertheless, was looking at me. He looked at me for a long time. Jaime had never looked at me a lot—at least until recently. In the past he seemed too young and too exuberant to look at people.

Ever since the Indian revolt, he had looked at me two or three times. And now he was looking at me, everlastingly.

"Felipe, you know what you have to do as I know what I have to do. We are as we are. I said that we were moving ahead in a hail of blunders. You told them what had to be said. We always say what we're doing. Our enemies have to be met head on. It's not good to wait for them. Everything must be done very frankly and very quickly.

"Let's now discuss ideas. Felipe, our enemies conducted themselves well. They assessed the situation accurately, in depth. They acted rapidly to forestall long-term consequences. They saw that my policies were challenging their beliefs and their interests. I want to renew the Indian people. As a statesman, I want that which is inevitable. Spanish blood has already been nearly wiped out in South America. It will be drowned. The Indian people will rise again from the terrible blow they received. They will adjust to and assimilate the way of life of their former conquerors. They will emerge from their indolence which is that of a sick person or a convalescent. From Mexico to Bolivia, such will be the case. I am only a precursor but I shall have many successors.

"These people know it. They know they'll be struck down as Spaniards, as masters and even otherwise. Florida knows that Christianity will succumb or be transformed. Belmez knows that wherever Christianity succumbs, the days of Freemasonry are numbered because it has never had the strength to provide its dream —which is to replace the Church—with serious social measures. The Masons are not cut out for replacing the Church. They are able and know how to act only in its shadow."

I interrupted again, "The day when the Incan empire is restored, something like the Incan religion will also blossom, to be sure. That conforms, of course, very closely to the Masonic dream which is, so it seems, to acclaim the religious spirit in all religions, to deliver the other religions from the exclusive and usurped predominance of Christianity, to refurbish Christianity with everything that preceeded, prepared and caused it—all these things without which it would not exist—with everything which, if forgotten, causes it to die in the long run. But you, Belmez, and those who lead you, you were unable to understand this in our thinking."

Jaime continued, "Therefore, Florida and Belmez felt they were left behind and they wanted to destroy me by what was to destroy them, by the Indians.

"Today, the revolt has been crushed and the dreadful harm that flowed from it will soon be contained. But that is something I will never forgive you."

Jaime was suddenly roaring. All of a sudden, looking at Belmez and Florida, he showed his hatred. He wasn't an aloof gentleman with elegant manners, he wasn't a dandy hovering between hypocrisy and cynicism; he was neither a gentleman nor a *caballero*—he was a man, just as passionate as he was contemplative, who wasn't ashamed of his passion. He detested his enemies and didn't hide it from them or from himself.

"You were treacherous and cowardly. Your association was monstrous. Treachery among yourselves as well as against me. You failed at the outset because you got frightened right away by what you had done. You then no doubt wanted to undo it and you wanted me to undo it. You acted like hysterical women. But Camilla had an excuse—she didn't understand what was going on, whereas you men should have understood."

I haven't tried to describe the shifting moods on these adversary faces during this long monologue. One of the accused was not a normal man: Florida. His expression remained impenetrable and in his eyes a constant flame was pulsating. An infernal flame, yet Hell includes more than half of the sky. As for Belmez, he was afraid and, in the long run, fear—repeating the same contortions—gave him a monotonous expression like Florida's. Camilla had again refused to show herself and had huddled down under the Indian cloak. The scornful remarks that Jaime showered on her did not make her shudder—perhaps because Jaime's voice grew soft and pleasing once they were said.

At this point, Jaime was attacking the accused too directly not to elicit some reactions. Florida said, "Will you grant me the right to speak?"

"I don't know," Jaime said, in a sudden outburst, just as harsh as the anger of the previous moment.

He slumped back in his chair and looked at the sky.

The sky—we had hardly looked at it all this time. But men indeed have the right to forget nature even though they are a part of nature itself.

I wanted to give some meaning to Jaime's gaze: "This is not a trial, not a verdict. There are neither accused nor accusors. We are opponents. He simply has the opportunity of setting up one of those meetings which are so unusual in the history of men. Entertaining meetings but which produce nothing, nothing. Napoleon's conversations with the Pope, with Metternich produced nothing. Each of us is too imbued with his subject. He knows everything that you can say. You also knew what he was able to say, at least externally. You don't grasp the originality of his thinking, otherwise you would be his friends and not his enemies. But furthermore, in a sense you are his friends. Our personal enemies are close to our hearts."

"Finally," Jaime continued, "after this Indian campaign that has cost me so much sweat and so many tears—my Agreda cavalrymen are Indians, executioners of their brothers! Bastards, all of you!—I needed a rest.

"Speak, Florida, but be briefer than I was."

"I am aware of the respect that I owe to power," Florida began. "Now your power has been tested and it exists. Undoubtedly you will not be assassinated, even if you have us executed. The Masons are the ones who started the revolt and not the Church which never begins anything. If I didn't stop the doctor, if I even helped him a little, that's because, Excellency, you are more on his side than ours. You are a Mason yourself, otherwise you could not have come to power. It was good for you to know your brothers. We were interested in bringing out this point.

"Concerning the heart of the problem, we shall discuss that later. That is, both our successors, yours and mine, will discuss it. You are young and you have thought too soon. That was already too much. It cannot be said that you acted prematurely because, all in all, you had done very little for the Indians before the revolt and you will do even less afterward. Your other plans will keep you from that. Because you *do* have other plans. Aren't you going to tell us about them?"

Florida was very glad to be able to speak. He took his time, got comfortable and planned on landing some blows. Hadn't he just landed one or two blows? This individual, incredibly futile in his strength, hovered over our destiny like a cat around a bowl of milk.

Jaime bellowed, "No, I won't talk to you about them. All this has gone on long enough. You won't be shot. One doesn't shoot institutions that the State can't destroy. I represent the State and the struggle between the State and the churches will last for a long time yet. It won't be over in 1968, neither in Europe nor in America. You will change or we shall change. One of us will absorb the other, at least for a while.

"What good would shooting you do? You would be replaced by others. You haven't been arrested, so you won't be released.

"I will detain only Doña Camilla.'

He ended with a truly free smile.

VIII

Belmez and Florida disappeared. Jaime had me stay with Camilla.

"We are going to spend the evening here."

The soldiers brought in some victuals and withdrew. Night had fallen.

We were again around the table, but Bolivia was no more than a few lights, born before the stars. Camilla remained unmoving and tight-lipped. We ate some fruit while drinking wine. Camilla refused at first, then, seeing us eat heartily, she changed her mind and began to bite into some peaches.

We stayed a long time without speaking until it was pitch black. Bolivia was these lights here and there in the dark. I lit a cigar, but Jaime stayed there with nothing in his mouth. We could hardly see each other any longer, for there was only a little bit of light on the table.

"It's all over between us, Camilla. It's been over for a long time. That ended as soon as it began. I told you that I loved you and I loved you for three days."

He fell silent.

"Love cannot last more than three days," I risked saying. "That is long enough for it to become eternal."

"Yes," Camilla said. "But you gave in to the temptation."

150

"I slept with you in your drawing room in La Paz so that everything could end as quickly as necessary."

"You shouldn't have."

"You wanted me to so much."

"Yes, but because you are so strong."

In the night his muted voice did not do him justice. His voice told of his helplessness.

"The good thing," Jaime's deep and calm voice continued, "is that we slept together again. When that no longer meant anything and could not add anything more."

"What you are saying is more idiotic than despicable," she exclaimed.

"No. The proof is that—of course, the sensual pleasure that existed between us was powerful, but I wonder what is that powerful experience. I said that sensual pleasure added nothing to what had been between us those three days, since that sensual pleasure didn't prevent you from betraying me for Belmez's sake."

"How are these things related?" she asked with disdain.

"That proves that our two beings, after having been rejoined, had been completely separated. You had become Doña Camilla Bustamente again."

"All right, but so what? The Bustamentes don't think like the Torrijos, that's all. What does this have to do with love?"

"Great God! That makes all the difference!"

She was silent a moment.

"Yes, that's where we really differ from each other," she continued, in a more intimate, more tender voice. "I loved the man, Torrijos, in you all along. I loved him sincerely and completely, and I love him still and will always love him. This man has nothing to do with the dictator you are now. There is a man in you like all others and yet different from all others, marvelously different from all others, not because he is a dictator, but because his name is Jaime. That is the man I loved. I loved him and you must know it, Jaime."

"Breasts of the Virgin!" I exclaimed next. "She's gotten even with you, Jaime. She's getting completely even with you. She forced her conception of life on you, their conception of life. They are individualists, as the English philosophers say. She loved you like an individual."

"She loved my shadow."

"Yes, Camilla," I ventured to say. "You loved a shadow. Jaime is a whole from which nothing can be taken without having everything die. Jaime is the body of a cavalryman, the soul of a hermit and the mind of a leader. He is his political ideas as much as the smell of his body hair or the way he kisses a woman; he is his friendship with all men and all women who love him and are his supporters. Jaime is everything or nothing: Jaime is Bolivia."

"Well, I love Bolivia as well as you."

"No, because you don't love Jaime, the Protector. But now Bolivia will forever be Jaime just as France is Napoleon and Germany, that you love so much, this Bismarck who has just won the battle of Sadowa and will create Germany in spite of Napoleon."

"Germany is Beethoven."

"No, it's obviously Beethoven and Bismarck."

"Filthy dog!"

"I am Jaime Torrijos' man. And you—aren't you Jaime Torrijos' woman?"

"Jaime Torrijos is womanless," Jaime grumbled, "and will stay that way."

I said again to Camilla, "Conchita is more of a woman than you. She's a whore but she never deceived him as you did."

"Bolivia is my woman," Jaime laughed.

"You're Bolivia's woman as well. The masculine genius of Bolivia fertilized your man of action's pliable soul. Bolivia and you are united. You are the perfect androgyny, having been brought together because you had already been reunited."

"You are saying strange things, Felipe."

"I have been telling you strange things, Jaime, ever since I met you and I had been saying them before I knew you."

"Who are you?"

"One half of yourself, as is each of us who follow you. Beginning with Conchita."

"I'm nothing then," Camilla murmured. "You're taking me very lightly. Nonetheless, Felipe, you went to look for me. You had a reason."

"The enemy has slept in my bed so that I might know him." Later, Jaime said, "Enough talking. Words spoken in the night are the only ones which have the same value as acts. Yet they must be brief like acts. A torch can be brought in now."

IX

As I was riding back alone the next day after lunch, I was going down the steep path which had taken all of us to Father Florida's retreat when my mare found herself nose to nose with a spirited stallion and myself with Ignacio.

Ignacio still looked at me with a terrible indulgence, for in his eyes I seemed so ridiculously fragile; yet, at the same time, I was Jaime's close friend.

"Don Felipe, why did you leave the retreat so quickly?"

"To be sure, it's a glorious belvedere, but—"

"When he left this morning, the boss told me to make you stay there. I went to see a girl nearby and I was really counting on your not being in a hurry to leave. You'll have to climb back—"

"But why?"

"You'll see."

He formed this silent and cruel smile that I had seen on his lips at certain times. Accustomed to the unexpected, I turned my horse toward the retreat. When we arrived, I thought that no one was there except us. The guards who were still on the grounds when I had left seemed to have disappeared.

Ignacio looked at me again and said, "There is only one person still here. The boss told me to leave you alone with this person and let you do what you wanted. There are many sheer precipices around here. You can also burn down the cabin. In short, it's up to you."

His silent smile widened. Then he turned his back to me and I saw him remount his horse and leave. Who could it be in the house? Camilla. That horrible and magnificent thought frilled my entire being and made all my veins pulsate. "Jaime gave me Camilla. He always knew I loved her, that I wanted her—as I loved and wanted Conchita. Since he doesn't want her any longer, he's giving her to me."

I was sure that there was nothing humiliating for me in this idea of my great friend—he had a feeling for fatalistic passions. Did he want me to rid him of Camilla as I had gotten rid of Don Benito for him—yet this time the blood would be directly on my hands? It would be just, for I had selfishly maintained an amateurish attitude in all these violent outbursts I had desired.

I looked around and listened. Alone. Alone, in this house, alone in the middle of this enormous mountain with myself, with the final reality of myself. Alone with my hands.

I didn't feel at all impatient. I looked slowly all around. I was on the terrace and I could see the flowers, the earth and the sky. I was alone as I had always been with the tools of my life in this lowly world: my guitar on the table, Bolivia at my feet with its sunny towns in the depths of the valleys so indifferent and so sensitive to my heart's whims, and the woman behind the door.

The eternally forbidden woman. Never had I cast my eyes on a woman—except for miserable Indian women, all miserable whores. If I should now raise my miserable eyes, one woman in the name of all women would spit in my face.

Or rather, would she beg me for mercy?

Would she fall to her knees? To save her life, would she give me her life—that life of life itself called honor? Beguiling, inexorable Jaime who had given me this present! After all, hadn't he wanted to humiliate me? Hadn't he wanted to get even with me? There is always a reason for getting even with a friend and didn't he have reason enough to get even with me for his entire destiny?

I waited, I kept a lookout, I listened. Nothing, not a sound. The whole enigma was unsolved. It was the enigma of my life. The enigma of one's life is even less decipherable than all the other enigmas. I was going to leave without looking, without knowing. What good would it do? Perhaps there was nothing and it was just a sad joke, played by a sad man on another sad man.

I lingered on the terrace. Dusk was coming in. I invoked the dusk. Little by little Bolivia was again lost in the depths. Soon, there would be only me with my destiny near the sky, more real than all Bolivia which had been nothing more than a diversion.

I took my guitar. Camilla was there behind the door. Did I love Camilla? Had I loved Camilla? My heart had only been ashes since the first day of my life, since I had seen my ugliness in a woman's eyes. Blessed ugliness which had made me learn early the essence of my heart and had destined me to my guitar. Camilla was nothing to me. I could do nothing with those admirable breasts, much less those of Conchita. Then again, maybe it was Conchita who was in there. Bah!

I could do nothing with Camilla's breasts, much less her soul. I knew Camilla's soul in which Jaime had found nothing. I held my guitar and began to play. I was playing. I suppose just then that I played well. Perhaps it's an illusion, for the artist was no longer there and whatever comes from the hands of a pure man is not perceived by other men. I played and sang. It was the song of desire and the death of desire.

I had to get it over with. I went quickly into the house. I opened one door, two, three doors. No one, nothing. It was a joke after all. I searched the whole house. I felt a great, sorrowful sense of relief. What might have been given to me here would have been a terrible enticement, worse than nothing. To have nothing was my lot, my manly lot.

I spotted a bottle on a table. I filled a glass and lifted it. That was nothing either, that was the delicious taste of the nothingness of this earth. I had never liked drunkenness. I drank. This wine had the unusual taste of a condemned person's wine.

"Well, Felipe, let's go." I headed toward the door.

Just then, I noticed a small chapel, hidden among the flowers. Father Florida's chapel. I opened the door, very much afraid I would find someone. And there, in fact, was Father Florida.

He was tied up, at the foot of the altar, his head turned toward the ceiling. A huge disappointment gripped me, a deathly weariness: that's all it was. Such had been, therefore, Jaime's thinking. A politician's thinking, insufficient thinking.

At least, I benefited from this by realizing, as I would never have done otherwise, that politics was the least of my worries.

I came up to Father Florida, bound and gagged. He saw me. Ever since Don Benito, I had known that it is not difficult to cause anguish in a man's eyes. Much better than metaphysics, a pistol or a gag. But I had seen this one crush his flowers and the other one chew on his cigar—signs of fundamental anguish.

I didn't hesitate. I untied the gag and rope knots and asked him to lean on me so he could get up and make it to bed. Naturally, he started to annoy me—straining, a second later, to smooth out his expression and regain his composure. I preferred his trapped-animal look in which it seemed there was more dignity. I have never seen man's dignity except in the sincerity of his passions. Thanks to this expression, a human relationship had been established between Father Florida and me, at least for a split second. I should be grateful to Jaime for having arranged this furtive interlude.

In spite of my liberating gesture, he didn't seem completely reassured. Irritated, I wondered if he ought to be. With a little encouragement, I might have regretted having set him free.

"Well, what are you going to do with me?" he finally said. "It now seems that the Protector's word was a lie. Or does he change his mind every two minutes?"

The audacity of that man, his eternal frivolity made my blood boil.

"I'm sorry," I said dryly. "Who tied you up?"

"A man who, I was told, was the public executioner."

"Yes, Ignacio. But Ignacio is also my friend."

"Congratulations."

"Bah, you deal with candle merchants. I find your attitude completely out of line. Enough of this foolishness. You're in my hands. Jaime has nothing more to do with this. We still have our personal matters to settle."

"Go ahead"

He was beginning to understand, and again in his expression anguish was easily triggered.

"We are alone in this house, Father," I added.

I had to give him, nonetheless, a true feeling for the way things were. Too bad if only crude tactics were effective—ridicule and pettiness—for they were being turned against him.

We gazed steadily at each other. Finally, there took place that authentic and healthy union of our souls which he had always eluded. Only once in a while do enemies as well as lovers reach one another this way. His passionately casuistic eyes let me count one by one the fiery coals which remained, weakened and shriveled, at the bottom of their dark, pulpy tar.

It was, all in all, everything I had ever asked of him and all that he had perhaps vaguely dreamed of giving me in his happier moments, beyond his passion for scheming—beyond flare-ups of modesty.

I had thought that I would find deep inside this house, with the aid of my friend, Jaime, an object of love and I had found an object of hate. Just as pointless. It reminded me of my adolescence when I was unaware that hate existed. Today I knew about this myth of middle-age after the myth of love. Father Florida was of no more use to me than Camilla. I didn't know what to do with him any more than I did with her.

But it was necessary that he not learn about this too soon.

"Do you at least know, Father, what are my grievances against you?"

He assumed, after a fashion, an exasperated expression.

"Circumstances opposed us."

"Father, you're cheating. Now it's your turn to confess your sins. Circumstances didn't oppose us in the least. We rearranged circumstances to favor our opposition. It's our opposition that is interesting."

The word confession had perked him up.

"My duty is to take part in contemporary events. I wouldn't be able to contend with them if I weren't familiar with the passions that govern these things. Passions cannot be understood without experiencing them."

"Without experiencing them—what rot! Admit that you experience them as well and better than anyone."

"That is possible. I am a great sinner, assuredly."

"Yes. I know that you must do penance standing in corners. But you would first have to practice the only true repentance which consists of replacing works of hate by works of love. You didn't make any effort to love me, Father."

A quarrel between enemies is frequently a lovers' quarrel.

"I had obligations toward you."

"Oh sure, but certain heinous acts weren't a part of your obligations."

"Which ones, my child?"

He had the nerve to call me his child. From the moment I had talked about confession, he had greatly recovered the attitude and tone of voice which were normally his.

"You made up your mind without any proof that I had assassinated Don Benito and coveted Doña Camilla. You played around with the souls of Don Jaime and Doña Camilla in this marriage project that you manipulated dishonestly. Without mentioning that along with Doctor Belmez, you are half responsible for the bloody Indian revolt. And there's probably more."

The burning coals were glowing again in his eyes. I turned my thoughts inward and considered the enormously unfair nature of my allegations. Hadn't I assassinated Don Benito? Hadn't I coveted Doña Camilla, all her sisters and Conchita? Hadn't I set up the meeting between Jaime and Camilla? Before the Indian revolt, hadn't I instigated Jaime's *coup d'état* and everything that was to follow?

The situation, in a second, was reversed. It seemed as though I were the one who was confessing to him. I was frightened by that. Not so much because of my weakening itself (this weakening had been foreseen from the moment I had untied him), but because of the result of this weakening. If I surrended to him, could I then decently let him go as I had first planned?

In all likelihood, my face was not as insensitive to my inner turmoil as it should have been, for in the dark holes of his eyes sparks were crackling more and more.

"My child, I don't know what you intend to do with me. But don't forget that I am a priest of God and before I die, I have the power to deliver you from your sins."

He was going a little too far. Although I was sitting in front of him, who was half stretched out on his bed, I stood up. The spell was broken. I had indulged myself enough in wild fantasies. I studied him again with the expression I had worn when I had entered the chapel and found him like a package on the ground. There where I had thought I would find a woman, nothing but a woman, I had found a man, nothing but a man.

"Father Florida, whatever the vast, legislative powers held by all religions and their ministers may be, you acted like a man with me and you will be treated like a man. You took a hideous interest in my life and you will be punished for it because I am going to kill you. See this pistol? Well, Father Florida, you're not going to die in a state of mortal sin, are you?"

Indignation had made me speak with a truly impressive determination. The burning coals died in his gaze in the saddest of downpours. His face collapsed, forever ruined.

"You think you're not in a state of mortal sin because you had taken care to confess your sins before coming to Jaime's meeting. Yet haven't you sinned since then? ... So, I don't know what the secret latitudinarian resources of your religion are, but you must surely consider it vitally important not to die in an unacceptable state. But a casuist knows better than anyone where the misuse of words begins and where the reality of one's thoughts ends. You're aware that for you any form of politics is a horrible sin and you're aware that you have sinned toward me through greed—you profusely desired my place at Jaime's side. ... Look what the absence of love does! If you had loved me, I would not have been able to resist you and I would have let you take that place."

Suddenly, he exploded, "But all I ever wanted was to love you. In the beginning, I loved you. You're the one who was ironical and disrespectful. You're just as evil as I am, I assure you. Right away you claimed that a guitarist is better than a priest—which was intolerable. And then you despised my chastity, which was a crime—especially on your part."

He dared say that to me. There would still be some venom left in him right up to the very last.

"Ah, you haven't seen within my soul either," he finished with trembling lips.

He was truly pitiful. Now that this objective had been achieved, I had no other recourse. Now it was knowledge, not pity, that was entering me. Perhaps it was a form of love. Suddenly rid of my quarrelsome self-importance, I entered him and saw him such as he thought he was. Between who he was for himself and who he was for me, the vague outline of who he really was took shape, in the eyes of some angel. For his sake, pray to that angel!

Thus, the arrangement I had dimly been looking for in this *tête-à-tête* had been concluded. First of all, I had been turned against this man by action, joyful action; then misunderstanding had rigidly set in, an unfortunate aftereffect of this action; finally, I arrived at a sort of knowledge and love which was primarily deliverance.

I concluded, "Look, Florida, we have been jealous, hateful. There is nothing in all that which isn't natural. Revenge is also natural. Within man's psychological make-up, it is often a necessary compensation. But for me, it comes too late. Leftover food has no taste. Ah, if I had just taken care of you before! You come too late just as Camilla might well have come too late. Killing you now would be a tiresome chore, without any resonance in my senses. I'm leaving. I'll have a mule sent to you from the next village so you can get back to La Paz. It is possible, however, that the irritation of seeing you again in La Paz may awaken manly feelings in me, animal spirits which are completely dormant at this moment. Here's hoping I'll never see you again."

I left on my horse along the well-used path. I finally seemed to understand the true meaning of the gesture Jaime had made in forcing upon me this *tête-à-tête* with my enemy. At times I had been critical of his activities as a man of action and I recalled that I had seemed to disapprove of his leniency toward his enemies a few hours earlier. He had wanted me to have full knowledge of the destiny that leaders must face.

PART IV

LAKE TITICACA

I

Once again, horses were at my door and it was a question of promptly leaving La Paz. This time, however, I had twenty-four hours to pack my things. As usual, Jaime's escort was very small. It was nighttime and we galloped away toward an unknown destination.

Outside town, Jaime slowed to a walk and, for the rest of the night, we rode slowly and silently. Jaime was deep within a calm meditation.

A lot of time had passed since the events I related. Jaime had made war on Chile and had lost because Peru had allied itself with Chile. The country, however, had not held its defeats against Jaime whom it had followed with ardor and had never disavowed.

In spite of constandy renewed intrigues, Jaime's power seemed assured for the rest of his life. He still worked a great deal and tried hard to repair the consequences of that unfortunate war. He succeeded in this rather easily, for our vitality was strong and the living promptly and joyously replaced the dead.

I had helped Jaime a lot during the war, but afterwards I had been rather withdrawn and had taken up my religious studies again. Jaime did not lose sight of me, however, and he was even more curious than ever about my ideas. He also had his own that he conveyed to me from time to time and which always surprised me.

We slept a part of the day, away from the road, and in the evening we started out again. Jaime told me that we were going to Lake Titicaca which is to the north, at the Peruvian border.

"I want to see that place once in my life."

I myself had never been able to go there, in spite of my great desire to see the ruins which are not far from the lake. These ruins were undoubtedly the true purpose of this trip.

During the second night, we walked side by side.

"Do you remember Agreda's march before the battle with Don Benito and that other march to cut off the Chileans from the Peruvians? Others besides me have failed in recent years. Lopez, in Paraguay, succumbed under the coalition of Argentina, Uruguay and

Brazil. Rozas had been unable before to prevent the separation of Uruguay and Argentina. The times are not ripe and maybe they never will be."

Jaime had aged and I knew that he had forsaken all ambitious projects. I had been astonished to see how, once the initial shocks of disappointment had passed, he had seemed to endure cheerfully the collapse of his dreams—to unite three countries into a federation as well as to begin the profound emancipation of the Indians. But, in the night of this trip, his voice took on a tone of excessive indifference.

"Is this southern hemisphere forbidden territory, perhaps? Is it perhaps outside of history? Will it possibly never shelter anything more than vegetative life? Of course, the plant kingdom has its moments of fury. ... Possibly, as well, I came a century too soon. Like Lopez and Rozas, like Napoleon and Bismarck. But the time for great deeds will return, for imperial deeds."

He didn't say much else to me until we got to Titicaca a few days later.

This lake is as big as an inland sea. It is a large eye watching the sky. Here, one is truly at the very end of Bolivia, land of extremes that can be compared only to Tibet. These are the final exaltations of mankind. There, man is too high up, already beyond himself. At four thousand meters, the sky—surprised in its immensity—is as deceiving as the sea, always naked, always empty, on the twentieth day of an endless crossing.

Here man can no longer be concerned with anything except the divine. Should the divine be the opposite of what is human, then this location could not be more appropriate. But, by the breasts of the Virgin, I do not believe that.

Here temples were raised near a lake, as in Tibet.

Supreme altars of the world. A race inscribes its measure of the divine. The highest measure. That measure had been taken before the coming of Christ's disciples. Here, one understands that Christianity is only one spiritual movement among others and there was no reason for it to come wandering up here. Travelers have made that observation in several areas of the world: Mexico, India, Tibet, China, Japan, the Moslem countries, Greece and Egypt. Whoever has sampled this feeling no longer enters a Christian church with the same perspective. He enters with a much more Christian awareness than someone who is familiar only with his parish and knows nothing about the five or six other great visions which gratify humanity.

There is an Incan religion—great, simple, destroyed.

The temple ruins are shapeless forms. Although grandiose and deeply painful for our South American hearts, for the heart of any human being whatever, they remain more terribly enigmatic than all others on earth.

Jaime and I had quickly gone there upon our arrival and we felt that miserly satisfaction of the traveler who clasps to his breast one of the planet's greatest testimonies and tells himself, "I hold it—at least I most likely have reached one of the sacred retreats of the marvelous house in which I live." He bitterly adds, "That's all there is. Here I am then at beauty's farthest limit." I suppose, at least, that certain travelers have that second impression. I myself have had only the first. Ah, to hold the earth! One holds the earth only when one of those points has been reached. The rest is merely incidental. The only living places are those places gripped by death. Life is reduced to itself, to a great solitary cry, a lost hermit's prayer, Robinson Crusoe's prayer.

For the first time, I was seeing a Jaime that I had never known, a Jaime who was no longer surrounded by men, a religious Jaime. On the other hand, I realized that this soldier had always been eminently religious. A great soldier is always a great ascetic.

Jaime and I were alone, among these ruins that dominate our country which is unaware of them. In a manner of speaking, no Bolivian has ever seen them. The world knows nothing about the Bolivian and he himself knows nothing about this lake, these temples, this place where his soul resides. This site might well be in Peru—that would also be unaware of it since they hardly value their own treasures. Here, thank God, the border was invisible and there were neither customs officials nor soldiers to make us notice it. That was good, for it is here that Peru and Bolivia are joined together as they were in the days of the Incas.

In a certain way, there were the best reasons in the world for Peru and Bolivia to separate the way they did under Bolivar's sad gaze. Reasons that were violently and exquisitely sensual, reasons that denoted life's special powers. Yet, in another way, how magnificent it was—the desire to want to reunite them, to attempt the impossible! An impossible that existed in the time of the Incas. We belonged to those men, Jaime and I, who need their homeland and other homelands as well. They are imperious men, imperial men.

Jaime came to the place where he had lived for years without having been there. He himself, a vanquished being, came to contemplate the victory he could never achieve. He was much more at home here than in La Paz. This great Bolivian also needed Peru. Thus it was that one day after Conception he had wanted Camilla. Then, he had gone beyond both Camilla and Conchita. At Titicaca he had passed beyond—beyond Peru and Bolivia, as for a long time beyond Conception and Camilla. There were no more women in his life.

The camp site was a long way from the ruins and Jaime and I were constantly in the ruins. It was then that we finally became aware of that double solitude we had known in Bolivia because no one sustained all of Bolivia like us.

On the second day, Jaime had gotten in the habit of coming to stretch out on the edge of a terrace whose jagged angle reached out like a thwarted desire over the immensity of celestial waters.

"Do you remember Camilla's balcony over the precipice at La Paz?"

"There was more giddiness on her balcony than in her soul."

"There were both Conchita and Camilla. None was capable of dominating the other, of absorbing the other. A man can collect a harem for himself but he cannot possess the world in a woman and not even in a nation."

"What is a harem compared to a nation?"

"And what is a nation compared to several nations? I felt big enough to love all South America."

"Are you Spanish or Indian?"

"I am South American."

"But what do you feel from your Spanish blood?"

A traveler told me that Spain was different from Europe, just as South America is different from the world.

"It may be a mirage of history but there are strange affinities, in our eyes, between Spain and South America. In the same way that

Spain is set apart from Europe, South America is set apart from the world. In the high Indian mountains, in the Cordilleras from Mexico to the Tierra del Fuego, there is something excessive and desolate as in the Iberian sierras. The religion of the Inquisitors and Jesuits could also be compared to those of the Aztecs and Incas. On both sides, you find autodafes, prodigious hecatombs, and the same frenetic cult of death in life. What we call revolutions, *pronunciamientos, coups d'état,* Protectors—is all this not the same incessant and inexhaustible search for earthly perfection we find in the blood of the Spanish as well as the Indians? This is why I am not surprised if we cannot tell whether you are Indian or Spanish."

We were speaking with great freedom. There was nothing more in me of that passionate and devious subordination toward him which had tormented me in the past. No further need for action kept him outside me. My guitar had been left at the camp site; all music was impossible in this place, too close to the gods.

"But what gods?" I exclaimed. "We don't know what these Incan gods were. You remember your youthful dream to restore the Incan empire. Undoubtedly I wanted you to restore the Incan religion. But what do we know about all that?"

"You're the one, Felipe, who put all these words in my head. What was I? A cavalry lieutenant who jumped on horses, handled a saber and rifle and wallowed in the love of soldiers and women. You put words in me."

"What was I? A guitar player, an insipid theology student. Suddenly you rose up before me—you were the form. The form. Being a lover of beauty, I rushed toward that form which was living beauty. Suddenly music and theology were a single being that was striding across the world."

"And you ask me what the word *Inca* is for me? You're asking me that? For twenty years I was this word *Inca* striding across the world, spoken by me alone deep within your heart. To me it seems that this word has relived and again meant something. Whoever wishes to find meaning in it has only to interpret my annals. The sweat and blood of men, the tears of women, the hooves of horses and the groaning of cannon wheels will bear witness."

"Yes, *Inca* means Torrijos. There is nothing more alive in human parlance than the name of a hero. Bolivia is alive only because of Bolivar. Did you think sometimes of Bolivar?"

"Never. That would have meant taking a rather meager pleasure in myself. No, I thought about heroes from yesteryear. About the most outlandish, about Alexander the Great, Genghis Khan, Tamerlane—about those who went beyond all expectations, those who reunited two continents. As for me, I would have been satisfied with half a continent."

"Well now, there are also Indians in North America."

"Let's stay within the limits of this lake which looks down upon South America."

"But this lake has no limits."

We experienced the bitter joy, the profound avarice of the traveler who has taken one of the treasures of the world in his hands and who repeats to himself, "At least, this is mine, this will never cease being mine. I shall have possessed one of the world's secrets. After that, I can look at the stars."

Jaime let out a horrible groan as he rolled convulsively on the temple basalt.

"Oh, woe is me! Oh, good for nothing! Felipe, I hate you. You are me and I am only you. Look! I am only a dreamer like you and an arranger of words. I wasn't able to conquer Lake Titicaca. I am only a peddler of dreams like you. I wasn't able to conquer Peru, to join it to Bolivia. I failed in my mission which is to make words come alive, to give form. If I had conquered Chile and Peru, today my capital would be built here, on the banks of this incomparable lake and Titicaca would mean something for all men. All these republics would no longer be small, charming and frivolous provinces; they would be an empire, something which uproots men from themselves."

"Forgive me, Jaime Torrijos. I served you poorly. I wasn't devoted enough. Every Agreda cavalryman did not succeed in dying three times for you. Yes, you had come to renew music and theology. You would have introduced a new form into the world. Inca would have relived as the word Roman has relived. What would Beethoven have done if Bonaparte had not shown him the way? I betrayed you and in betraying you, I betrayed music. Music needs great forms which rise up on the horizon. Shakespeare owes everything to Elizabeth, and Goethe would not have written the second *Faust* if he had not had the French Revolution before his eyes. Give us great men and great deeds so we can find again the meaning of great things. Each hero nourishes ten great artists. Goethe and Hugo dipped their pens in the blood shed by Napoleon. Today in Germany, Wagner and Bismarck are marching to the same cadence; yet they are not aware of each other."

"It's a great joy to think that Bismarck has avenged Napoleon I for Napoleon III," I added.

Then, digressing, we said no more that day except little nothings that made us laugh.

II

Ideas on art, I was thinking the next day, are not the only ones which are dipped in the blood shed by heroes. Of course, that is already a lot—that is enormous. For example, at Buenos Aires a magnificent work has just been born which will always honor South America, the *Martin Fierro* by Hernandez. He is indeed the brother of Lopez, Rozas and Torrijos. After the Homeric siege of Montevideo which lasted ten years, this sublime poem came into being which is the last epic written by men and incrusts a diamond into the crown of age-old Spanish literature. But religious ideas are also those which are dipped in the blood shed by heroes. Gods as well as poets need sacrificial blood in order to exist.

I had occasionally gone to see Tamila again on his mountain. I knew that Jaime had been there as well. When I returned the first time, it was because I had in mind the sorcerer's words about Belmez: "They know secrets that the Indians know better than they."

The "secrets" of Belmez and his ilk were those of Freemasonry. I thought I knew what their true value was. The Masonry is even closer to and farther away than the Church from certain truths that a few pure hearts discover again in each century, guided by a confused, disappointing, yet valuable tradition that seems secret only because of the ignorance and indifference of most people.

I had questioned Tamila, and Tamila had not answered me. Perhaps he had nothing to say, or perhaps his entire treasure consisted only of a few magical practices that he didn't fully understand.

Had there been in the ancient Inca religion true secrets, true mysteries as in other ancient religions? Had these secrets been kept? If Tamila didn't possess them, did he know some Indians who possessed them and whom he didn't want to expose?

I was leery of myself, of the weariness I had encountered in my theological research and leery of the sort of revolt that took hold of me as a result, putting me at the mercy of a completely romantic seduction. Hadn't I developed, during our wars and the negotiations that were intertwined with them, an automatic taste for secrets which are really not, but concocted only by the most fortuitous intrigue?

I had given up putting direct questions to Tamila. Involving myself in his most humble practices, I had tried, getting progressively closer, to grasp a thread which possibly might have led me back to his principles, if he had any. But I didn't go far, and there always came a time when he stopped talking. Then, his wife would hum, and they would both lose themselves in a state of taciturnity which was perhaps the only possible quality of their art.

He was seeing Jaime. Did he tell him more? Jaime, however, didn't have the analytical ability that I possessed, the knowledge of words, the subtle habit of words. Perhaps action, the excessive responsibility of action had made him capable of reaching some key mechanism which was overlooked by my indolence, my incurable solitude?

I had climbed back alone onto the terrace and I saw dust on the temple steps and in that dust the blood Jaime had shed in his wars and which was there to revitalize the basalt of the old temple. By whatever means, the word Inca relived through this blood.

It was not in vain that the form of Jaime Torrijos had risen over Bolivia. But, in the dwelling of the gods, the form of the hero had to be specified. The form of the hero would invoke the form of the god. If the hero were to rise solemnly in the temple by means of a serious and long invocation, the form of the god would reappear.

"The ritual, the ritual. The ritual has to be performed again. In the temple of his ancestors, the hero, who combines the blood of the Inca conquerors and the blood of the Spanish conquerors, the hero, who carries in his veins a new baptism and a new sacrament, must link his religion with the previous religion. The new is born of the old, of the old which was so young.

"Our life—Jaime's and mine—is ending, but it has not been fulfilled. Now, it must be fulfilled by prayer and sacrifice."

This idea, which filled my heart with pity and tenderness, had come to me from a dream I had had during the night. I had relived a scene I had witnessed during the Indian revolt or during the war with Chile. It was in a destroyed village, inside a church in ruins. There was nothing but blood and ashes everywhere. In the church there was only one section of a wall left against which an altar was still leaning. In the early dawn a priest was celebrating mass. The sacrifice in the ruins. The sacrament regained its full significance. Life and death were joined together in that offering, that victim raised by the priest. Eternal gesture of all religions, sacrifice—the gesture of sacrifice which only collects and stylizes the gesture of life. Man is born only to die and he is never so alive as when he is dying. But his life has meaning only if he gives his life instead of waiting for it to be taken from him.

That was the only mass that I could accept, me the musician who had become a warrior, who was a warrior like my ancestors—me, the man of Torrijos, the war leader. At the foot of the altar, there were only soldiers. They alone had the right—the sacrificed, the sacrificers —to attend this sacrifice; they alone brought it a guarantee, a sanction. No women, only some warriors and a priest. The women were crying and giving birth elsewhere. Elsewhere, they had their own mystery which matches that of men.

A god dies and is reborn; man dies and is reborn. Perpetually, he creates forms in which he is reborn. These forms fix their essence first in war and religion, then in art. While attending that mass, I had in my hands the masterpiece of Hernandez, the *Martin Fierro,* the gentle and virile lament of the unhappy gaucho, the manly lament of the warrior and shepherd of the pampa. That above all was our South

American psalm which was just as valid as the psalm of the ancient warrior and Hebrew shepherd.

"We are going to make a sacrifice," I said to Jaime.

"We have made many already."

"You don't understand me—a sacrifice as the Ancients used to make."

He looked at me a moment, then said very slowly, "Yes, this is perhaps the time. What kind of sacrifice will it be? And to whom?"

"The sacrifice will not be made to God, but to one of the gods, to our god."

"The god of the Incas?"

"No, we are too ignorant of Incan lore. Of course, I have questioned Tamila a great deal, but either he doesn't want to tell me everything or he doesn't know a lot. ... There was the Sun God for the common folk and behind this god, an Unknown God for the even more credulous ones. 'Blessed be the innocent ...' We said that Incan lore was the lore of Torrijos. Rather, let's say the substance."

"Why?"

"I'll explain theology to you in another life."

"You were my living book."

"What is the god who expresses the substance of Torrijos?" He didn't understand. Yet I had had another dream during the night. The Agreda horsemen—a few old veterans who had survived the war with Chile—were burning in our camp fires a wood they had brought and which exhaled dreams. I had seen Jaime on a horse that was turning its back obstinately to me as it walked. That had distressed me, but also given me an idea.

"Your god is your horse."

He seemed shocked.

"Your horse is the only possible image of your god. Therefore, we shall sacrifice a horse."

He did not understand.

"You were the outstanding colonel of the Agreda regiment. You were a centaur, a leader of centaurs. You have galloped over the highest plains in the world. You loved horses, didn't you?"

"I worshipped them."

"How easily you admit it; yet the war horse that you worshipped, as you say, was sacrificed in the charge."

"Alas!"

"To whom were you sacrificing it? To the idea of Inca, to the idea of Torrijos. As a result, the best thing you can do for your god is to sacrifice his own image to him. To your god the horse, you will sacrifice a horse."

All of a sudden, my man seemed very moved: "Felipe, you don't know how right you are. Yes, it's time for me to sacrifice my horse. My own horse is the one that must be sacrificed."

He had come on a magnificent stallion, which was not a road horse and that had astonished me.

"Yes, it's a stallion. That will do fine."

"You say that we shall sacrifice my horse, Brave, to the god of Horses."

"To the god Horse."

Once again, he was displeased.

"This is a guitarist's—a poet's idea. You're just reciting one of your poems for me."

"Yes, I would sing, 'The Agreda cavalrymen have been swept away on horses of fire, far from women, into the sun—.' Yes, but one day in a camp of ours you said to me, 'There is nothing prettier in the world than a horse. It would be better to make love to mares than to women.' The image of your god can only be that which seems the prettiest in the world. The Christians say that God who became man is in the consecrated bread and wine. We are going to consecrate your horse through sacrifice."

In the evening, we set out with Ignacio and the horse, Brave. During the day I had made the necessary preparations. The chosen place was the large inner courtyard of the temple. A pyre had been built there.

At the last minute, Jaime told me that he missed his men. So, I went back to the camp to fetch the men. They came. They all had Indian blood and they squatted around us.

The full moon was spilling into the sky. Next to the pyre, Ignacio was holding Brave who was unsaddled. Jaime took out his dagger and said to the men, "Agreda horsemen, our wars are over. I don't want my charger to grow old in a stable."

One can never tell men the precise truth because they would not understand. There was just then a lie or mystery in our religion as well as in all others. But at least we were aware of this, whereas Catholic priests no longer know what fall, incarnation, redemption, holy sacrifice, Holy Spirit mean. They had constructed a petty and mediocre moral tale from these terms which are, however, a great metaphysical poem.

A long murmur went up from the men.

Jaime said then, "Felipe, sing the song of the horses of Agreda."

I sang without my guitar. The men took up the refrain in thickly broken tones.

Then, Jaime moved forward and embraced Brave on his nostrils, on his eyes, and plunged the knife into his neck. Brave's mane stood on end and his hooves drummed a ferocious plea against the earth. Sprawling on the ground, he fought against the inevitable. After that, it was all over. We turned the pyre over on his body and set it on fire.

Then, by themselves, the men sang an Indian song that I knew well. It was to this funeral rhythm that Conchita had danced in the palace.

Suddenly, I understood that all the past was dead and Jaime would not be going back to the palace. What is a Bolivian palace to the man who has dreamed of South America? Bitter is his homeland to the one who has dreamed of an empire. What is a homeland to us if it is not a promise of empire?

And so, now, we had entered a region where the very idea of empire was gradually fading.

When the fire had expended itself in a cruel odor of burnt flesh— that odor with which we had been saturated in our wars—the men stood up. Before leaving, they all came to gather closely around Jaime for a moment. They were seeking his hands and kissing them and squeezing them. They were crying. They were crying over the end of their youth and the consummation of their glory.

We saw them move away, one by one, among the ruins. They did not know that they were treading on the glory of their ancestors.

Jaime and I remained seated near a pile of foul-smelling ashes. That was what we had wanted.

We were exhausted and satisfied. I had put forth a good idea which had extended and completed the idea Jaime had first had of this pilgrimage. We had solemnized, we had celebrated, we had sacrificed.

Of course, I thought to myself, the sacrifice of the horse does not exclude the sacrifice of the mass and we could have a mass in this temple at daybreak. In this temple devoted to the Sun, we would see the golden ostensory raised in the dawn's rays. The Incas were deeply aware that God was behind the gods and there was the unnamable behind the horse and behind the sun.

Being familiar with the universal and fundamental theory of sacrifice, they were familiar with the sacrifice of the mass which is only one of its aspects.

But all that would take too long to explain to Jaime who, furthermore, had lived through all that. For who will honor God who sacrifices himself if it isn't the sweat-covered hero?

We remained in the temple wrapped in our cloaks and we slept near each other, next to the ashes of our double destiny.

III

"I am going to leave, Felipe. I won't be going back to La Paz."

"Yes, I understood last night that you would not return to La Paz. I thank you for having brought me here. Have you left instructions in La Paz?"

"I designated Fernandez as my successor, unfortunately!"

"Yes, unfortunately. The people won't accept him. Fernandez loved you, but too narrowly. He won't be obeyed when you're no longer there to command him. He's boring, inept, and he will be overthrown."

"Whether I step down today or in ten years, it will be the same."

"That's true."

"I can no longer give anything to Bolivia except prosperity."

"That will prepare the way, perhaps, for someone else later on."

"You shouldn't ask too much of me."

"Or rather, one shouldn't ask less of you than you can give."

"My time is up."

I didn't want to ask him what he was going to do. I was waiting for him to tell me.

"I am going away alone toward the north, toward the Amazon.

"You're going to enter inexorable wastelands."

"That's possible. When I was a child, I dreamed of these unknown regions. I will be the man who has attempted all his dreams. After all, I didn't have so many."

"They say that Inca fugitives took refuge in there four centuries ago."

"Perhaps."

"No one can approach them."

"Who knows?"

I said nothing more to him about that. I was not astonished. That man who had astonished me was no longer able to astonish me, and that was no doubt why he was leaving. We were no longer at an age when one astonishes or is astonished. Each of us could no longer function except through customary channels.

"Do you remember Don Benito? I had forgotten him for a few years. Now I've been thinking about him again."

"Yes, I'm acting a little like him. I certainly owe him that. He was a man of complete discretion."

We ate dinner in camp with the men as if nothing were wrong. But the men were deathly sad. If they had known, they would have wanted Jaime to take them with him. Yet, they would have preferred death to exile, for what can a simple man do far from his homeland? Even a man who attempts to scale the heights always longs for his homeland. Jaime would long for his homeland and myself as well.

Jaime left on foot. He had taken very little baggage, no weapons except a knife. I went with him outside the camp. He allowed me to walk by his side for an hour.

My heart was heavy, and I suddenly wondered why Jaime would not allow me to go with him. What harshness! How harsh he had always been with me! But I had loved him poorly, served him poorly, and friendship must be consummated like love.

Moreover, he was forsaking himself and so he really had to forsake me as well. It was no longer a question of him nor of me nor of us. It was a question of something else.

I cried and he cried as well. That did me an awful lot of good.

I had cried two times in my life since I had become a man—when I had discovered my ugliness in the eyes of a woman and the day when I had understood that we had lost the war and the empire would not come about.

We were crying so hard that we sat down.

"The age of empires will come. Take heart, Jaime."

Much later, he said, "I was loved and I loved a lot. A lot of blood and tears were shed for me. I shed some as well and I shall now give everything that I have left."

"Jaime, don't leave me!"

"You will leave Bolivia and go to Europe. I've set aside a little money for you at La Paz. You will go and see everything you love over there and you will write about everything you have loved here. You will bear witness."

He added, "You must know, old fellow, that we can no longer do anything for each other. We belong to those who want to die with their eyes open. It's time that we cease to exist for each other as for everything we have loved."

I felt another surge of futility and curiosity. I asked him, "Are you going to join up with the Incas?"

He shrugged his shoulders. We cried some more. But, in the long run, we grew tired of crying. Then, he was able to leave.

I gazed at the back of this man behind whom I had walked for twenty years. The man on horseback was now on foot.

EPILOGUE

I found this manuscript in my grandfather's affairs, hidden away in his country home. I remember that he had often talked to me about one of his old friends, a South American—a Bolivian or Patagonian: he hardly knew the difference—who lived in Paris like an eccentric in a student's room cluttered with books.

That man, in spite of his wild appearance and fierce passion for strumming his guitar and hoarsely singing too mild or ominous chants, had a certain cultural background. He haunted the *Comédie Française* and concerts and it was here that my grandfather, intrigued by this solitary man, had met him.

When old Felipe died, there was no one at his funeral, except my grandfather and a few strange characters that he didn't know. His books were auctioned off, but my grandfather, out of a sort of pity, had collected his papers. He had stuffed them in a crate, and afterward forgotten them in his attic.

My grandfather suspected that this wild man was probably an impostor, not a South American but a Spaniard from Spain, a political refugee.

What would he have said if he had read the manuscript, entitled, *Excerpts from the Mémoires of Jaime Torrijos, Written by His Brother*? In fact, there was no Jaime Torrijos according to history, and this story, which contains some monstrous inaccuracies, seems to have been written by someone who never set foot in Bolivia, but, at the very most, has dreamed of doing so.

THE END

AFTERWORD

For the English-speaking reader, *The Man on Horseback* is undoubtedly one of Drieu's most accessible novels. In terms of comparable quality, it ranks among the best he ever wrote. Whereas other novels, such as *Middle-Class Illusions* or *Gilles,* are broader in vision and more overtly autobiographical in content, *The Man on Horseback* by contrast is a work of contained dimensions, far removed from the traditional Parisian settings that Drieu seemed to fancy. Centered around the rise to power of Jaime Torrijos, a Bolivian strongman of the late nineteenth century, it is a skillfully executed, fast-paced work whose plot moves deftly from one episode to the next without letting the reader's interest wane.

It is more, however, than just a well-constructed adventure story. In its own way, *The Man on Horseback* serves the same "experimental" purpose as the other "confessional" novels by permitting Drieu to objectify and analyze a basic antinomy within himself–the opposition between the contemplative and dynamic aspects of his character. By underlining this fundamental division of his personality, Drieu hoped to discover in the evolving relationship between the two main characters (each of whom incarnates one of the polar attributes–thought and action) some unforeseen perspective on the nature of his true being. At the same time he was delving into this dichotomy of self, Drieu was also seeking to clarify the reasons for his adherence to fascism. In the rise and fall of the Bolivian dictator, Torrijos, Drieu was alluding, on an allegorical level, to the corresponding rise and decline of European fascism over the previous two decades.

Although *The Man on Horseback* is essentially the anatomy of an ideological failure, it is also a work of vicarious fulfillment in which Drieu tries to compensate for his political misjudgments. Just as Jaime Torrijos–the military leader Drieu himself had always longed to be–will abandon his dream of restoring the ancient Inca empire in South America, Drieu in turn recognized that the German armies under Hitler would never bring about the unification of Europe that he had anticipated. In the final scene of *The Man on Horseback,* this disillusionment with the fascist regime is effectively sublimated. The messianic leader–or fascist demi-god–is transmuted through ritual sacrifice into a legendary presence for future generations to emulate. By sacrificing his charger, Brave, to the concept of military heroism on the shores of Lake Titicaca where, centuries before, the Incas themselves had offered human sacrifices to their sun god, Jaime symbolically renounces his imperial aspirations and withdraws from war and politics into exile. Thus, in this ascetic retreat from the world, Drieu gives by association a compensatory value and dignity to his adherence to the fascist cause.

As the critic, Frederic Grover, has pointed out, the disappearance of Jaime Torrijos into the Amazonian wilderness is not only indicative of a change from hero to saint but can also be symbolic of a martyr's fate. In light of his identification with Judas Iscariot in *Straw Dogs* (Drieu was also at this time writing a play about Judas to be called, "The Man Who Hanged Himself"), it seems obvious that Drieu considered his role as a collaborator and fascist militant to be an ultimately sacrificial one. Fully aware that his participation in the Collaboration would prove fatal, Drieu chose, in his life and fiction, a martyr's death over prudent compromise. In the same manner that the poet, Felipe, at the end of *The Man on Horseback,* will recount the legendary feats of Jaime Torrijos and glorify his name, Drieu also found solace in the belief that his works and exemplary death would bear witness to the legitimacy of his political commitment in the eyes of posterity.

Other than Torrijos, the most significant character in *The Man on Horseback* is the narrator, Felipe. Contrary to Jaime's iron-willed heroism, Felipe is portrayed as a vacillating and multi-faceted personage—ex-seminarian, poet, guitarist, confidant and *alter ego* of the emergent strongman. In Felipe, we find a striking portrait of the "man of contemplation" (*l'homme de rêve*) who is clearly more representative of Drieu's own character traits than the fiery man of action as found in Jaime Torrijos. By isolating his penchant for abstract thought and meditation in Felipe, Drieu felt he could come to grips more effectively with this "undesirable" tendency which had kept him, so he thought, from realizing his full potential. The bayonet charge at the battle of Charleroi had revealed his true self to be a dynamic whole uniting thought and action and transforming fear into courage. Having experienced in these euphoric moments something akin to a mystical revelation, Drieu was convinced from then on that, deep within him, lay the aptitude for forceful and heroic leadership. To his dismay, neither war nor politics nor sensual love could ever provide him with the same sense of oneness—of being a *complete* individual in every respect—that he had felt while charging toward the machine-gun emplacement. In the long run, Drieu would be forced to acknowledge the primacy of his intellectual bent. It was therefore the scholar, *le clerc,* and not the warrior, *le guerrier,* who would triumph in this struggle for inner unity.

Although the final episode of *The Man on Horseback* is characterized by the recognition of defeat and the separation of the two companions, there is a moment of symbolic unity that occurs between Felipe and Jaime, following the sacrifice of the war horse, when both men are made aware of just how inextricably bound they are to one another. Without the guiding hand of his mentor, Felipe, Jaime Torrijos could never have come to power in Bolivia; without the man of action's dynamism and courage to give form to his ideas, Felipe in turn would have remained a frustrated dreamer, strumming his guitar and singing of the deeds of other men. This symbiotic union of thought and action, however, is only fleetingly realized. Having divested himself of all military and political power, Jaime withdraws from the world of action into solitude. Alone as well, Felipe will then go abroad to bear witness through his works to the fame and accomplishments of the now legendary hero who was once an integral portion of himself. Therefore, in *The Man on Horseback,* Drieu bids farewell to the concept of the heroic leader—which for years had been the driving force behind his political militancy—and turns toward religious meditation and art in his quest for self-unity.

In addition to the reconciliation of thought and action, *The Man on Horseback* illustrates quite well another recurring theme in Drieu's writings—that of misogyny. Whereas this negative attitude toward women is evident throughout Drieu's earlier works (especially in *The Ladies' Man* and *Strange Journey*), the female characterizations in *The Man on Horseback* seem to be by contrast unusually heavy-handed, even caricatural in their vulgarity. The two categories of women Drieu portrays are decidedly unflattering: the haughty aristocrat of questionable virtue, Camilla Bustamente, and the sensual prostitute, Conchita, dominated by her immediate desires. Even Camilla's younger sister, Isabel, although well-intentioned, has few redeeming qualities. In the end she follows her own self-interests and betrays Camilla for the sake of her lover. As Jaime will conclude after his retreat from power and women, there was no appreciable difference in a moral sense between Camilla and Conchita. They were both on an equal footing in the art of willful deception. Promiscuous, egocentric to a fault, and treacherous—women in Drieu's eyes, seemed incapable of noble acts. Having no penchant for sacrificing themselves to a higher cause, chained to their baser instincts, they were in every respect the antithesis of the heroic spirit.

There seems to be no readily apparent explanation for Drieu's misogyny. Although his two marriages ended in divorce, he remained nevertheless on very good terms with his former wives. In fact, it was his first wife, Colette Jeramec, who was so solicitous of Drieu's welfare after the Liberation of Paris and who provided him with funds and hiding places until his suicide. During the last ten years of his life, Drieu had formed a somewhat trying yet durable relationship with the married woman he called "Beloukia" and who had been the subject of an allegorical novel by the same name in 1936. As an inveterate womanizer, Drieu was obviously unable or unwilling to accept the long-term emotional commitment of marriage with its mutual obligations and restrictions on personal freedom. In one of his more candid moments of self-analysis, Drieu confessed that, in effect, he had deliberately pursued women in order to flee Woman herself. In his opinion, therefore, love was not a fulfilling experience based on tenderness and mutual respect but a sensual prelude to desertion and profound anguish. The traumatic episode with the American diplomat's wife, Dora, in *Gilles* is a perfect example of Drieu's belief that love was no more than an evanescent mood, destined to end once the initial passions had been spent.

Even if we choose to interpret Drieu's philandering as an attempt to reject domesticity and preserve his individual freedom—in brief, the consequence of a certain adolescent mentality—this still does not fully explain why, in all his fictional works, Drieu managed to create only one truly sympathetic female character—Genevieve Le Pesnel of *Middle-Class Illusions.* In his diary and elsewhere, Drieu freely admitted his misogyny and at times even seemed to delight in making preposterous statements about women that he obviously knew to be exaggerations. If we exclude from consideration certain Jungian overtones of Mother-hatred as the source of Drieu's antipathy toward women (moreover, by his own admission, it was his father who inspired his hatred, not his mother), a correlative hypothesis can then be proposed which has serious merit—namely, that his misogyny was in essence a form of self-rejection inasmuch as he tended to see in the women he courted and seduced (and subsequently wrote about) those very qualities he himself possessed but was unwilling to tolerate.

Those who knew Drieu well often spoke of his alleged "feminine" character traits. In this respect, his enemies even went so far as to accuse him of latent homosexuality (i.e., Jean-Paul Sartre) in his obsessive, almost erotic quest for power and the virile strongman. One of Drieu's last short stories—the semi-autobiographical, "Journal d'un délicat" ("Diary of a Delicate Soul")—explores the labyrinthine vacillations of the "delicate," creative temperament which seems to hang from the neck of the narrator like an albatross. In this perspective, it would appear that Drieu viewed his artistic sensibilities as an impediment along the way to self-unity.

Since Drieu's novelistic technique (using himself as a primary model for most of his characters) demanded an unavoidable "self-distancing" or esthetic objectification of fictional subject, it was impossible for him to bring about unification of the divided self from within the creative consciousness. Once scrutinized, the self simply fled Drieu's probings into myriad shapes of which no two were alike. In a paradoxical sense, Drieu's success as a writer of exceptional ability was nonetheless an outward sign of his failure to merge the contemplative and dynamic attributes of his personality into a virile whole. Whereas this proved in the end to be an unreasonable goal—totally out of keeping with his temperament—Drieu had made such fulfillment the focal point of his existence. It was his untimely lot to feel "incomplete" because he lacked the aggressiveness and singularity of purpose needed to be a leader of men.

To the extent that women served as mirror-images of Drieu's own deficiencies (or those characteristics he interpreted as faults), the negative portraits of women that abound in his works are perhaps the result of an unwillingness to accept the limitations imposed by his "effeminate" qualities and literary talents—in brief, a form of revenge exacted upon himself. If this analysis of Drieu's misogyny is correct, then many of his inconsistencies and compensatory acts would stem from the need he felt to give himself a more "masculine" dimension in order to counter the effects of his essentially contemplative nature.

In this vein, however, the question also arises if Drieu would have been driven to create with the same intensity had these inner antagonisms and their resolution not acted as a stimulant to his art. At any rate, by searching for a means to bridge the gap between thought and action, Drieu was very much in line with the activist concerns of his generation. As children of Nietzsche's messianic prophecies and call to action, they were no longer satisfied with observing the world around them and sought to lead a more vigorous and at times dangerous existence.

As we mentioned earlier, *The Man on Horseback* is a novel which attempts to define and justify Drieu's motives for adhering to the fascist cause. In this capacity, it is undoubtedly a work of ideological import—an allegorical and self-indulgent defense of his political beliefs. As soon as he realized that fascism had failed as a vehicle for European unity, Drieu turned to the novel in order to clarify his own relationship to the movement as well as symbolically reconcile his inner duality of self and give the whole, tragic adventure an ideal conclusion. For this reason, Jaime Torrijos is portrayed not as a reactionary, but as a strongly progressive leader championing the common people's demands for social and political justice. In opposition to Jaime's populist stance, the conservative strongholds of Bolivian society band together in a desperate effort to maintain their privileges in much the same way that their European counterparts did in the thirties to stem the tide of fascism. As a consequence, the Church (represented by the Jesuit priest, Florida), the landed aristocracy (Camilla Bustamente) and the Freemasons (Doctor

Belmez) refuse to compromise with Jaime's regime which poses a threat to their traditional pre-eminence in Bolivia. Just as Hitler and Mussolini first garnered support for their cause among the lower middle-class elements whose social and economic well-being had been threatened by severe inflation and parliamentary instability, Jaime appeals to the dispossessed Indians whose land and freedom were long ago usurped by the Spanish conquerors. Because Jaime himself comes from the people, his plans to restore the Incas to their former grandeur has a legitimacy and historical urgency that cannot be neutralized by his adversaries. In spite of his mistress' duplicity and the concerted opposition of the ruling classes in Bolivia, Jaime eventually triumphs over the conservative bloc and reigns supreme within the confines of his native land. Similarly, in its formative stages, European fascism easily took root in those countries where political conditions favored its growth. However, as it passed inexorably into a militaristic and imperialistic phase, fascism began to decline as a movement of social revolution. In a parallel fashion, Jaime tries in vain to extend his influence militarily into neighboring states, meeting with defeat at the hands of the Chileans. In 1942, the year in which *The Man on Horseback* was written, fascism had reached such a point in its decadence.

Although a variety of opinions have been expressed concerning Drieu's motives for adhering to fascism, no one explanation seems entirely satisfactory. In part, this is the result of Drieu's own changing attitude toward his political options in relation to an ideology which itself was in constant evolution. At the time of his original commitment to fascism in 1934, Drieu was unquestionably motivated in his choice by a desire for profound institutional and moral change throughout Europe. In his eyes, fascism was the needed authoritarian force that would purge France and other nations as well of their rationalistic heritage which had unjustly separated mind from body, weakening both the individual and national will to power. In a symbolic sense, Drieu called for the death of France—that is, the destruction of parliamentary democracy and the creation of a fascist state whose primary function would be to eradicate decadence and revitalize its citizens.

Other than the need to combat decadence in contemporary society, another reason for Drieu's militancy in the fascist ranks—in particular his role as editorialist for *Emancipation Nationale*, the P.P.F.'s weekly organ—was perhaps the nostalgic wish to experience again the virile camaraderie of the trenches within the solidarity of a collective movement. In spite of his initial enthusiasm, Drieu was progressively disillusioned with the fascist movement in France. In 1939, Drieu saw Doriot at last for the impostor he truly was ("just another Radical Party politician," Drieu wrote in his diary) and resigned from the P.P.F. in disgust. On the other hand, in November 1942 (after finishing *The Man on Horseback*) Drieu rejoined Doriot's party when such a gesture was politically meaningless and fraught with danger. Although he would later justify his decision to rejoin the P.P.F. by stating that he wished to humiliate the German occupational forces with this public rejection of their half-hearted efforts to implement a true fascist government in France, he also added, in a most revealing assertion, that he hoped his presence on the podium with Doriot would infuriate his enemies and give them ample reason to kill him later. Thus, in light of this admittedly suicidal act, it does seem plausible that Drieu's true motive for remaining faithful to a moribund fascist movement was a deep-rooted compulsion to destroy himself. Assuming this to be true, we can then establish an analogy between the self-negation implicit in misogyny and the self-destructive wish openly expressed in his allegiance to fascism. Since, in Drieu's hierarchy of values, woman occupied a mediating position between man and a knowledge of universal oneness (or the Continuum of the Brahmanic mystics whose writings heavily influenced Drieu, especially during his last years), her presence—like Drieu's own artistic temperament—was thought to be an obstacle to his aspirations of self-unity and spiritual transcendence. To a large degree, the ultimate dependency he developed upon the sexual mediation of his partner (herself an indispensable conduit to the deep rhythms of the universe) was for Drieu a form of humiliation inasmuch as he became painfully aware of his inability to escape from himself without the intervention of an outside force. As Drieu concluded in *Straw Dogs*, his penultimate novel, the will to transcend oneself and perform heroic deeds (i.e., the Nietzschean ethic) had been vitiated by an all-pervasive decadence. Instead of serving as a means of mutual fulfillment, the sexual act is described in Drieu's novels (with very few exceptions) as a struggle for dominance between the male aggressor and his female victim. Drieu's misogynistic tendencies, therefore, led him to envision women as distorted or even caricatural versions of his own so-called "negative" qualities. Thus, by rejecting womanhood in these fictional portrayals, Drieu was consequently denying an essential portion of himself. All things considered, it stands to reason that this refusal of his female counterpart constitutes a form of affective suicide—a subconscious wish to destroy himself emotionally by withdrawing from the world into a vicarious and perhaps illusory self—that of the charismatic hero.

In an analogous fashion, Drieu's commitment to fascism was originally inspired by the wish to destroy the decadent self through political and moral reform and thereby let a new being rise from its ashes—less analytical, more intuitive and dynamic in character: a modern Dionysus tempered by a watchful Apollo. In the same manner that the individual consciousness would die and be regenerated within the fascist ideology, France itself would expire as a political entity and rise again, phoenix-like, within the confines of the fascist state under German hegemony. Ideally, therefore, both the divided self and the French nation would be made whole again and restored to a mythical equilibrium that the Middle Ages had supposedly achieved.

For the most part, Drieu's misogyny and fascistic preference resulted from his inner division and unceasing quest for a more robust and complete personality. In the long run, however, his bold schemes to reconcile thought and action failed. There would be, he realized, no "total" individual free of decadence, no idyllic social order cast in the mold of a less fragmented epoch, no virile elite to lead the masses to their destiny. In the final years of the war, Drieu confronted this overwhelming reality with lucidity and despair. As *The Man on Horseback* eloquently affirms, the era of romantic fascism and its cult of the heroic leader had come to an end.

Thomas M. Hines